Cross-Check!

Cross-Check!

Lorna Schultz Nicholson

James Lorimer & Company Ltd., Publishers
Toronto

James Lorimer & Company Ltd. acknowledges the support of the Ontario Arts Council. We acknowledge the support of the Government of Canada through the Book Publishing Industry Development Program (BPIDP) for our publishing activities. We acknowledge the support of the Canada Council for the Arts for our publishing program. We acknowledge the support of the Government of Ontario through the Ontario Media Development Corporation's Ontario Book Initiative.

Cover illustration: Greg Rhul

The Canada Council | Le Conseil des Arts
for the Arts | du Canada

ONTARIO ARTS COUNCIL
CONSEIL DES ARTS DE L'ONTARIO

Library and Archives Canada Cataloguing in Publication
Schultz Nicholson, Lorna
        Cross-check! / Lorna Schultz Nicholson.

(Sports stories)
ISBN 978-1-55028-969-5 (bound)
ISBN 978-1-55028-968-8 (pbk.)

I. Title. II. Series: Sports stories (Toronto, Ont.)

PS8637.C58C76 2007   jC813'.6   C2007-900352-4

James Lorimer & Co. Ltd.,	Distributed in the United States by:
Publishers	Orca Book Publishers
317 Adelaide Street West,	P.O. Box 468
Suite 1002	Custer, WA USA
Toronto, Ontario	98240-0468
M5V 1P9	
www.lorimer.ca	

Printed and bound in Canada.

CONTENTS

For Grant Nicholson,
my hockey hero

Acknowledgements

I'd like to say thanks to my son Grant Nicholson and all his hockey buddies. I go to so many tournaments because he plays minor hockey. I even went to Quebec for the Pee Wee tournament. A big thank you goes to Mike Rout from Kelowna Heat Hockey. He is paving new ground by giving out my novels as MVP awards at their Kelowna tournament. Many thanks to Jeff Hunt, with the Ottawa 67's, for promoting my books. And to John Grisdale, at the BCHL, for using my books in their Read and Succeed programs. I also have to thank NHL player Dany Heatley and Wayne Gretzky for loving this great game and supporting my book. I'm truly honoured. Lastly, I want to thank the Lorimer team for letting me write about hockey, and to you, my readers, for reading my books. Enjoy! Please visit my website at www.lornaschultznicholson.com.

1 Pre-Game Excitement

The room was completely black when the clock radio alarm went off. Five-thirty. Josh Watson immediately sat up and rubbed his eyes. He had time for a quick shower to wake up.

A rustling sound made him reach for the bedside lamp. The hotel room lit up: two double beds, a big dresser, a mini-bar, and a television console with movies and Nintendo. Josh's dad stirred beside him. On the other bed, Josh's friend Tony Seeley was trying to disentangle himself from the rumpled sheets.

"Dibs on the shower!" Josh yelled. Tony tried to tackle him when he sped by. Mr. Watson groaned. "You can have the shower first tomorrow!"

Josh playfully checked Tony back onto the bed and ran into the bathroom. He picked up the little bottle of body wash from the wicker basket on the counter, and stepped in the shower. The hot water soaked his red hair and he closed his eyes, letting it trickle down his back.

When Josh's alarm went off for school, he always pressed snooze and stayed in bed as long as he could. Not today. Not the day he and his hockey team, the Calgary Rockies, were about to play their first game at the Kelowna International Bantam AAA tournament.

As he soaped himself he sang as loudly as he could: "We are the Champions."

★ ★ ★

The brisk winter air sent shivers through Josh's body. Kelowna wasn't as cold as Calgary but the air still had a nippy bite. The early morning sky was still as black as a puck. With heavy hockey bags slung over their shoulders, Josh and Tony headed across the hotel parking lot to the van, which was already breathing out fumes. They threw their bags in the back. Josh hoped his dad had the heater on full blast.

"Your track suits look smart," said Mr. Watson when Josh hopped in the front seat.

Both boys wore the same black Rockies outfit. The team had made enough money with fundraising to get a fleece-lined winter coat, matching wind-breaker pants, and two mock turtlenecks, one red and one black, for each player. The best part was the black-and-red toque with the long ties. Josh liked the fact that the suits were in the team colours of the Calgary Flames.

All the way to the arena, Josh stared out the window, going over the season in his mind. So far, playing AAA hockey had been quite different from playing on his old team. The guys on his team had come from all over the northwest of Calgary, instead of just his community, and most were fourteen-year-olds. Josh and Sam Douglas, his goalie from last year, had been the only thirteen-year-olds to make the team, but Sam had played less than a month before he had to move to Ontario with his family. Josh had been a bit lost on the team without his best buddy. He was glad he had Tony from his old team to chum with. At the beginning of the season Tony had been cut from the Rockies because, although he was skilled, the coach thought he was just too small. But when one of the guys had quit, Tony had been called up to play. Josh was convinced Tony should be on the Rockies because he could lay as good a hit as the big guys.

Josh could see the bright lights of the arena. It was a twin arena and the tournament games were being played on both sides. The gold medal game would be played in the Prospera Arena, home of the WHL Kelowna Rockets. Josh sucked in a deep breath. He couldn't think about that game yet; he had to focus on today's game against the Kelowna Stars.

"Thanks, Dad," he said as he pulled his equipment out of the car.

"Yeah, thanks, Mr. Watson," Tony said. His voice

sounded hollow. Josh turned to glance at him. The look on Tony's face echoed the nervousness in his voice.

They entered a quiet dressing room and found two spots together on the far side. Tony sat on the end of the bench and Josh sat between him and Nick Bell, the captain of the team.

"Hey, Red," said Nick. He'd given Josh the nickname at the beginning of the season — because of his hair, of course. Nick's own sandy-coloured hair was sticking straight up. He leaned over to unzip his bag. At fourteen, he was already broad and muscular — all set to follow his oldest brother, Brent, into the NHL. Brent played for the Vancouver Canucks. Josh had a personally autographed picture of him hanging on his bedroom wall at home.

"How are you feeling?" asked Nick, glancing up from his bag.

"Great," replied Josh.

Nick was always concerned about Josh's diabetes, not that there was much to worry about. A couple of months ago, Josh had switched to an insulin pump that let him administer his own doses. It was handy, though he didn't like wearing it on the ice. He left it behind in the dressing room and took a power drink out to the bench, in case his blood sugar got too low.

"That's good," said Nick. "Hey, you played with Kevin Jennings last summer, didn't you?"

"Yeah." Josh grimaced, remembering Kevin all too well from elite hockey camp. He was one of those guys who thought he was cool.

"Is he as great as everyone says?"

"He's good," replied Josh. "But he's a hot-head and a real jerk. If you get him mad, he might take some dumb penalties."

"That's important info. Thanks for the tip. I want the gold medal." Nick had a hard look of determination in his eyes. "My brother's team lost this tourney in the final, so I want to win."

"We will," said Josh, hoping he sounded confident.

"I have a strategy. In every game I have to stop the best player. If I do that, we'll win." Nick sat tall and held up his fist for Josh to hit.

As they did their team handshake, Josh felt shivers run up his spine. Nick was so serious. Could they win? Josh bent over and pulled his skates out of his bag.

2 Important Game

Josh stepped on the ice full of energy. He skated a few fast laps then got down on the ice to stretch. Tony followed Josh.

As they did their groin stretches, Tony asked, "Which one is Kevin Jennings?"

Josh scanned the ice. "Number 33." Kevin had to have added ten centimeters to his height since Josh had last seen him.

"He's big."

"Yeah. It looks like Kelowna has a lot of big guys." He grinned at Tony. "Don't worry, we're little but tough."

Nick skated by Tony and Josh. "Time for warm-up," he said.

During warm-up Josh went over in his mind what coach had said in the dressing room. This first game was an important one to win. It would set them up for the tournament. If the Rockies kept winning they would get a better schedule, fewer games. Josh took his place on the bench with the other players on the second line. Tony and the rest of the fourth line were down the bench a bit. The Rockies first line was on the ice. Josh leaned forward with his one elbow on the bench and watched as Nick and Kevin lined up at center for the face-off. *This should be interesting,* he thought.

The puck dropped and the two centers battled at centre ice. Nick kept pushing Kevin, but Kevin managed to get his stick on the puck and flip it back to his defence. Nick charged forward and, on his way, gave Kevin a slash to the pads. Kevin turned and jabbed him back.

Nick's aggressive fore-check made the Stars' defence turn over the puck. With the puck on the end of his stick, Nick skated forward. Kevin pivoted and hustled back, trying to catch him as he went deep along the boards. Josh was itching to get on the ice and, since he didn't usually play the penalty kill, he hoped that Nick wouldn't do something stupid to give the Stars a power play. Both Kevin and Nick roughed it up, but the puck got rimmed along the boards and sailed behind the net, where it was picked up by the Stars defence. When it was fired out past the blue line, Nick skated in for a line change. As Kevin passed him, heading to his bench, Nick slashed his pads again. Kevin scowled at Nick.

The play had turned over again and was in the Stars' end zone. When his winger came in for a line change, Josh stepped on the ice and skated like crazy toward the Stars' net. He anticipated the pass between the Stars' defence and somehow managed to get the puck on the end of his stick. He was close to a breakaway!

Then he felt the hit. Josh had discovered that Bantam hockey was tough, the hits hard. He braced himself and managed to stay on his feet. He knew he couldn't drive to the net, so he looked up, saw his linemate out front, and made a pass. The puck slid toward his forward, who fired a shot on net.

When Josh came off, Coach John patted his back. "Good work out there, Josh. You played tough and solid."

Josh nodded his thanks and took his place on the bench. He watched the play go up and down the ice, both teams evenly matched.

Nick was on fire. He flew toward the puck, picked it up, and skated hard to the net with Kevin right on his heels. Nick held out his arm to keep Kevin away as he drove wide. Relentless in his attack, Kevin kept on Nick, hooking his stick around him. The whistle blew. Josh clapped his hand on the boards. Yes! Kevin had a penalty, and Josh could tell from how he shook his head that he was angry at the call.

Nick skated beside Kevin as he made his way to

the penalty box. Nick's mouth was moving non-stop. Josh had no idea what he was saying, but he knew it would definitely annoy Kevin. Nick was one of those players who liked to pester the opposition with his constant chirpy chatter. Josh thought Kevin was going to take a swing at Nick, but he held his cool until he got to the box — then he slammed his stick.

"Power play, boys!" Coach John glanced up and down the bench. Josh held his breath. Usually, he didn't play the power play. Would he today?

"Cycle the puck," said Coach John to Josh, patting him on the back.

Yes! Josh blasted on the ice and skated toward his wing. This was his chance to prove himself. When the puck dropped, there was a scramble. Josh moved in for support. The puck landed on the end of his stick, so he slapped it back. His defence picked it up and passed it over to the other defence, who sent it down along the boards to Josh's opposite wing. The Stars were playing the penalty kill box well. Josh moved toward the side of the net, hoping he could hit a deflection or pounce on a rebound. His centre, James Zahir, moved wide and the winger passed to him. Josh skated in front of the goalie to screen him. The goalie swatted him with his stick. The Stars' defence pushed Josh, trying to knock him off his feet. Bracing his body, he stayed strong on his skates.

James fired a low wrist shot to the right corner.

The puck zinged past the goalie and into the net! Before Josh could jump in joy, he felt a shove to his back and fell face-first on the ice. James skated right over and pushed the player who had shoved Josh. The ref flew into the circle, spraying ice. "Break it up!" he yelled.

Josh got up and adjusted his helmet. "Awesome goal!" he said to James.

"Thanks for the screen."

Josh skated to the bench as Kevin was let out of the box.

"Tell number 12 that I've got his number," Kevin muttered to Josh.

When Josh got on the bench he turned to Nick. "He told me he's got your number."

Nick smirked. "That's what I wanted."

Coach John patted Josh on the shoulder. "You're playing smart hockey, Josh. I like that."

★ ★ ★

After two periods the score was still 1–0 for the Rockies. Josh and his teammates filed into the dressing room.

Josh took off his helmet and leaned against the wall. Sweat dripped from his face like water from a leaky faucet. He turned to Tony. "You're doing great out there."

"Thanks," said Tony. "It's so much faster than the hockey I've been playing. You've improved a lot playing on this team."

Josh felt he was playing the best hockey he'd ever played. After he had rested for a few seconds, he glanced at Nick, who was wiping his face with a towel. He turned when he saw Josh looking at him.

"You're kicking butt, Red," said Nick.

"Thanks. You and Jennings are really going at it."

"I've been waiting for the right time to nail him." Nick clenched his teeth. "He better be ready. If I nail him and get him out of the play, we win our first game."

After Coach gave his dressing-room pump talk, Nick put his helmet on and snapped up the chin strap. Then he stood up. He motioned for his two assistant captains to stand as well. The dressing room hushed.

"We can do this, Rockies!" Nick spoke with determination. He scanned the room, looking each player in the eye. "Let's put the Stars in their place. We're a team and we can do this together." Josh had never had a captain like Nick, someone who could control the dressing room.

The Rockies headed back to the ice. Josh was still on a high from Nick telling him how good he was playing. This period he had to keep up the intensity.

Every time Josh stepped on the ice he skated and checked hard. In the Stars' end, he fore-checked, creating turnovers. And he almost scored a few times, but both times he was robbed by the goalie. Every time he came off the ice, his breathing was so rapid he had to sit for a few seconds.

The tension between Nick and Kevin escalated during the third period. The score was still 1–0. Josh looked at the clock. Two minutes left. His line had just been out so his chances of playing again weren't looking good. Coach always shortened the bench and Josh was usually the one to sit.

All the guys were standing to take in the last minutes of the game. Even though it was a morning game and the stands were only half full, tension filled the arena. The clock ticked down a few more seconds and the Kelowna coach called in the Stars' goalie. The Kelowna fans went crazy.

"Josh!" yelled Coach John. "Get ready."

Josh looked up in surprise.

"You're the next forward out." Coach put one foot on the bench and yelled, "Darren!"

Darren hustled toward the bench.

"Go, Josh."

Josh raced toward the play. Both Nick and Kevin were out. Kevin had the puck and was heading toward the Rockies goalie. Nick was on him. Josh knew he had to fore-check and support Nick.

Nick tried to knock Kevin off the puck. Josh barrelled in and levelled Kevin against the boards.

Kevin didn't fall, but he did lose control of the puck. It skidded behind the net. The Stars' defence picked it up.

Out of the corner of his eye, Josh saw Nick quickly look around before he lifted his stick and cross-checked Kevin from behind. Kevin smashed into the boards and went down.

The fans started screaming. "Hey, Ref, watch the hit from behind!"

The ref and linesmen had been too busy watching the play behind the net. They had missed the hit and kept the game in play. Josh was stunned. He knew it had been a dirty hit. If Kevin stayed down they would have to blow the whistle. Suddenly, the buzzer went. The game was over.

Josh watched Kevin slowly get up. Nick skated over to Josh and slapped him on the back. "One down," he said. "You deserve a star for today's game."

Josh grinned uneasily. He had played the best game of his life, and his team had won. He should be happy! He watched Kevin skate toward his net doubled over in pain.

3 Reunion with Sam

"Hey, who wants to go and trade pins?" Nick pulled a big Calgary Rockies pin out of a red felt bag, stood on the dressing-room bench, and waved it in the air. "Our pins are going to be hot because we're going to the gold-medal game!"

All the guys burst into loud cheers. Nick was so convinced the Rockies were going to win! Josh had never played with anyone who was more determined to win than Nick — or anyone who was a better captain.

"I can't wait to trade my pins." Tony yanked on the gold drawstring to open his red bag. He pulled out a pin that had *Calgary Rockies* written across it. The background was a blue sky and mountains. Hockey pucks dotted the sky like stars, set so that they actually moved back and forth.

Trading pins was one of the highlights of this tournament. Josh had heard that from the guys who attended before. Each Rockies player had ten big pins and twenty little ones. Josh had scratched his initials on the back of his pins. If he made the NHL one day, those pins could be worth a ton of money. Tony had laughed like crazy at him.

After the noise level had dropped, Josh turned to Tony. "I'm going to trade my small ones today. I'm saving my big ones because we're going all the way." He hoped he sounded as confident as Nick.

"I'll do that too." Tony bobbed his head. "We should hurry so we can see Sam play. He's on the ice right now, in the other rink." Tony whipped his jersey over his head.

"It will be great to see him," said Josh. He'd really missed Sam when he'd moved to Ottawa. Now he played net for the Kanata Kings. Josh was looking forward to seeing Sam play.

Josh and Tony the were first to leave the dressing room. As they were walking down the hall, Tony asked, "Is Nick always such a dirty player?"

Josh shrugged. "Not always. The guy is so skilled. You should see him snipe the puck to the top corner."

"He knocked Kevin from behind," said Tony, as if he hadn't heard Josh. "He's lucky he didn't get kicked out of the tournament. That hit could have cost him three games. And us the tournament."

"What did Coach say on the bench?"

"I don't think he saw the hit. It wasn't near the play. You know, Nick's brother hits hard but he doesn't play dirty."

"Nick says he doesn't want to be like his brother. He says he has to be known for something else." Josh knew he sounded like he was making excuses for Nick. "Nick just wants to win."

"Nick doesn't have to play dirty to be different. His brother is known for his finesse. Nick could be good at laying hits, but not dirty ones."

"He can lead a dressing room."

"Yeah, I'll give him that," replied Tony. "But—"

"We should stop talking about Nick," said Josh quickly. "There's Kevin Jennings."

"Do you think he'll remember you from camp?"

"Probably not."

Josh and Tony sped up to pass Kevin. They were almost by when Josh heard his name. He cringed.

"Watson," said Kevin.

"Hey," replied Josh, turning around. He tried to act cool.

Kevin walked toward him, scowling. He stood in front of Josh and flicked his blond hair out of his face. Josh had to look up at him.

"Your team is dirty," said Kevin. He crossed his arms. "Number 12 should have been kicked out."

"The refs didn't call anything."

"That's because they didn't see it, but I felt it." Kevin uncrossed his arms. "It was a cross-check from behind, Dude."

"When's your next game?" Since Josh had read the schedule at least twenty times, he was well aware when Kevin's team played next. But he really wanted to change the subject.

"Six tonight. You guys will probably play the Edmonton Arrows. That Inuit kid you roomed with at camp last summer is on that team."

"His name is Peter Kuiksak, and he's the best Bantam player in Canada," said Josh. He liked Peter, and they had kept in touch through e-mail. Peter had moved from the North West Territories to Edmonton so he could play hockey.

"He's warming up right now in the rink we just played in." Kevin flipped his hair again. "His team is on the ice in a few minutes."

Josh turned to Tony. "We'll have to go in there after we watch Sam."

"That's your goalie friend from camp, right?" Kevin asked.

"Yeah," replied Josh.

"I bet he's the best goalie here."

Josh nodded, thinking that for once Kevin had said something he agreed with. Maybe Kevin was over his anger.

But Kevin's face broke into a web of furrowed lines. "I'll get you guys back, you know," he said. "Somehow. You might have won this game, but I bet you'll get knocked out from being in the box all

25

the time or from having suspensions. We're going up the back side, right to the finals. This loss means nothing."

"We should go, Josh." Tony interrupted. "Or we won't see Sam."

When Josh and Tony were out of Kevin's earshot, Josh exhaled. "How mad was he?!"

Tony raised his eyebrows. "He's kind of got a reason to be cranked."

Josh glanced at Tony. Why was he so down on Nick? They were on the same team. It wasn't as if Nick got a penalty.

They walked through the arena lobby, heading for the other rink. Josh saw his dad and waved to him. "Sam's playing!" he called out.

Mr. Watson halted Josh. "What a great game, boys!" Josh could tell his dad was happy with how he had played. He was always positive, but today he had that proud-father look.

"Thanks, Dad." Josh beamed.

"Tony, I thought you fit in real well with this team."

"Thanks, Mr. Watson."

Mr. Watson checked his watch. "Coach John wants you back at the hotel by two to rest and get ready for tonight's game. Meet me back here by one. That gives you two hours." He rested his hand on Josh's shoulder. "Do you need money? I see some of the boys have scarves to put their pins on."

"I've got enough for food but not for a scarf."

Mr. Watson pulled out his wallet. "Tony, do you need money to buy a scarf? I could lend you some until we get back to the hotel room."

"No, I've brought enough with me."

Mr. Watson gave Josh some money and he patted him on the back. "Have fun. Say hello to Sam for me."

"I will."

Inside the rink Josh looked immediately at the clock. With only ten minutes left in the game, Kanata was leading 5–2.

"Come on! Let's go down by the glass." Josh ran down the stairs, holding his red bag of pins close to his body so he wouldn't drop them. As soon as Sam was off the ice they would start trading. And Josh would grab something to eat. It had taken Josh almost a year to get his diabetes under control, so now eating the right amount at the right time was almost automatic.

After a few minutes of watching Sam's game, Josh turned to Tony. "He looks good!" Sam was agile and technically skilled, and he played the angles well. The puck rimmed out of Sam's end and Josh smiled as Sam stood up for a breather. Sam batted both posts, and Josh almost laughed at the familiar gesture. He always did that.

Suddenly, the crowd started yelling. The puck had turned over and a player from the other team was heading toward Sam on a breakaway.

"He's coming out of his net," said Tony. "He still plays aggressive."

"I wonder if the guy will deke or shoot. I'd deke and go for his five-hole."

"Yeah." Tony held his hands about a foot apart. "Sam has a five-hole this big."

Josh laughed. "You got that right. His weakness for sure."

They watched as the skater deked and tried to pop in a shot on his backhand. Sam stuck his glove in the air and snagged the puck!

"Some things haven't changed!" Josh grinned. "Sam still loves the Hollywood save." Josh turned and jabbed Tony. "I hope I get a breakaway on Sam. I'll shoot low and right through that big space." Josh mimed taking a wrist shot.

Sam had definitely given his team the winning edge and the Kanata Kings played around with the puck until the game ended.

"Let's wait for Sam in the lobby," said Josh after the buzzer went. "We'll scout out the trading environment."

Josh noticed that a lot of the guys trading pins were players from the hometeam Kelowna Stars. They wore dark green suits, and their jackets had a big gold star on the back.

Josh bought a scarf and a sandwich. After his last bite, he wiped his mouth and grinned at Tony. "Let's trade now," he said.

Tony and Josh approached a group of boys. At first they stood on the outside, feeling a little shy to move in and ask if anyone wanted to trade. But then a boy looked at them and said, "Hey, you're from the Calgary team."

"Yeah," replied Josh.

"I've heard you've got the coolest pin." He pulled out a big Alaska Huskies pin. "You want to trade?"

Josh inhaled. The Huskies were a middle-of-the-road team, not really hot, but not losers. What would their pin be worth? Now that he was in the midst of this trading stuff, he was tongue-tied. "Um."

"I'll trade with you," piped up Tony. His eyes were lit up and his grin was gigantic as he pulled out one of his big pins.

Josh watched as Tony traded with the guy from Alaska. As they walked away, Josh whispered, "What happened to saving the big ones?"

"Look at this pin!" Tony lifted his scarf to show Josh the Alaska pin. It had a sled dog playing hockey, and the dog's tongue slid back and forth. "It's so funny."

Josh laughed and playfully pushed Tony. "It's kind of stupid."

Tony made the dog's tongue go back and forth. "It's hilarious."

Tony and Josh burst out laughing. Then Josh said, "They could have had the dog peeing. Now *that* would have been funny."

"Or —"

"Hey, Josh! Tony!"

Josh turned and grinned. It was Sam. He looked the same, with his mop-like blond hair and permanent smile. And he didn't look as if he'd grown at all. He was with another kid, and they both wore burgundy jackets with *Kanata Kings* emblazed on the front in gold. Suddenly, Josh stopped smiling. It was weird to see Sam in something other than a Calgary jacket.

Josh had been so excited to see Sam, but now that Sam was standing in front of him, wearing another team jacket, Josh felt strange. What if Sam had changed?

"Good game!" Josh couldn't think of anything else to say. "That was an awesome save you made at the end."

"It was a Hollywood!" The dark-haired Kanata King shouldered Sam. He had a low voice already and some zits, and he was big — way bigger than Sam, Josh, or Tony. Josh wondered if he was already fourteen.

Sam laughed and pushed back, although his impact didn't do too much. Sam's friend was built like a brick. "I'll get you, Becker."

As Josh watched Sam and Becker horse around, he felt as if he was watching a movie, watching from the outside instead of the inside. Josh used to be the one horsing around with Sam.

"First game down, Hollywood." The Becker guy put Sam in a headlock.

"But not our last." Sam squeezed out of the head-lock and stopped fooling around long enough to look at Josh. "You guys won too, I heard."

"We beat Jennings' team. Remember him from the summer?"

Sam rolled his eyes. "That guy thinks he's so good."

"I heard your captain nailed him from behind," said Becker. Josh still didn't know Becker's first name. "Someone said he should have been kicked out for the entire tournament."

"It wasn't that bad." Josh shoved his hands in his pockets. "Jennings whines a lot." Josh wanted to forget about the hit from behind. "Peter Kuiksak is playing right now," he said. Did his voice sound too high? "We should go watch him."

Sam glanced to Becker, almost as if he wanted to check with him. This surprised Josh. Sam never did that with him. Josh and Sam usually just did things instead of consulting one another. And if they didn't agree, it was no big deal. They just did their own thing.

Becker shrugged his shoulders. "Sure," he said. "Is this the guy from the summer camp you went to? The one who is so good?"

"Yeah," said Sam. "He rifles his slapshot. My hand would sting after I caught one of his shots."

"You mean after you Hollywooded it. Let's go. You know, see our competition."

Becker started walking toward the rink and Sam

followed. Josh sped up to walk beside Sam. Tony fell into step beside Josh.

Josh opened his red pin bag. "You want to trade, Sam?"

Sam pulled out a gold felt bag from the pocket of his jacket. He looked at Josh and grinned — Sam's old grin. Josh grinned back.

"I heard your pins are really awesome." Josh heard the excitement in Sam's voice.

"Don't trade any big pins now, Dude," Becker called back over his shoulder. "Remember what we said in the dressing room."

"Oh yeah," said Sam. "Here." He pulled a little pin from his bag.

What was with Sam? Why did he do everything his new teammate did?

4 Reunion with Peter

"Did you see that shot?" Josh slapped the glass.

Peter had wound up and fired a wrist shot so hard that it hit the top corner of the net and bounced back out. His team was winning 4–1 in the final minute of the second period. Peter had already scored a hat trick. At this rate, he would win tournament top-scorer for sure. Josh wished he could play hockey like Peter or Nick.

"That goalie didn't even see it!" Sam exclaimed. "He threw up his hand when the puck was already in the net."

"That Peter guy is a clunky skater, but he can shoot," said Becker. Josh had finally heard Sam call him Steven, but he couldn't stop thinking of him by his last name.

"I think he's a good skater," said Josh. "He might look rough but he's fast. Every now and again he gets tangled up but he's got so much power in his legs.

They're the size of tree trunks. Did you see him fly by that guy? I heard he already has an agent, and next year he'll be drafted for sure." Josh wondered if he was talking too much and too fast.

"Are you kidding?" Becker furrowed his brows. "An agent?"

"Yeah. There was a story in the newspaper about how he moved from the Northwest Territories to play hockey in Edmonton. I think he's like the first kid his age to ever get an agent. Usually that doesn't happen until second year Bantam."

The buzzer sounded to end the second period. Becker jabbed Sam and pointed to the stands. "Look at all the guys trading pins up there. Let's go see."

Sam turned to Josh and Tony. "Come on."

Josh felt like a tag-along. He shrugged at Sam. "I might stay down here."

"I'll go!" Tony grinned.

"Seeley, at the rate you're going, you'll trade all your pins in one day," said Josh.

"Nah. I've got a strategy."

"Come on, Josh." Sam shifted from side to side before he lightly hit Josh in the upper arm with a left hook. Then he bounced back as if he was sparring. Josh and Sam pretend to box in the halls at school all the time. "And it's a right hook to the left shoulder."

Josh sparred back. "And he gets a left hook to the gut."

Sam doubled over. "I'm down." He flopped to the floor.

Tony jumped in as if he was the ref and started counting down.

When Sam straightened up, he said, "Let's go up top."

"You're on." Josh held up his thumb.

Josh ran up the stairs behind Sam to the landing. A big group of guys were showing each other their pins and making deals. In the middle of the gang was Kevin Jennings.

Tony walked right up to the circle.

"Look at Seeley," said Sam. "He's right in there."

"I know," replied Josh. "I bet he has no pins left by the end of today."

"Ours are okay." Sam yanked open his bag and pulled out a pin in the design of a crown. "The crown means Kings. Get it?"

"Duh. Of course I get it."

"They're kind of lame if you ask me." Sam grinned at Josh. "A kid on our team thinks he's some great artist, and he designed them. Let's do that trade now."

Josh stuck his bag behind his back. "How good is your team? I don't want to trade if your team is lousy."

"We're awesome! We're going to win it all."

"Yeah, right. You won't beat us."

Sam tilted his head and looked at Josh. "It's so weird not to be on your team anymore."

"Do you like Ottawa?"

Sam shrugged. "Yeah, it's okay. My school is huge. I still get lost."

"You got lost in our school and you had been there since you were in kindergarten." Josh laughed.

"Look. That Kevin guy from summer camp is coming toward us," whispered Sam.

"He looks as if he's still cranked from our game. Let's get out of here. Peter is back on the ice. Let's watch the rest of his game."

Josh and Sam almost collided as they bolted away from Kevin. Josh laughed and jostled Sam. Sam pushed him back. Then they ran toward the stairs.

"Let's sit here." Josh flopped into a seat in the third row down. Sam sat beside him.

"Is Kevin still a hotshot?" Sam asked.

"He's pretty skilled." He glanced at Sam. They had always been honest with each other. "Nick *did* cross-check him from behind."

"Nick Bell?" Sam asked.

"Yeah."

"I watched him play Triple A last year. He's not a dirty player. His brother has already scored twenty goals for the Canucks. He should just learn from his brother."

"He doesn't want to play like him." Josh paused. "I don't know what he was thinking. Nick's a good guy. He's been my only friend on the team since you left and Tony got called up." Josh watched Peter smoke a guy against the boards. "Now *that* was a good hit."

"Peter is amazing."

"He was written up in *Alberta Hockey Now.*"

"Sweet. We don't get that magazine in Ontario. Do you think Peter's changed from being so famous?"

"I dunno. We should go see him after he's finished his game." Josh glanced at his watch. It was only noon. "I'll have time. We have to be back to the hotel by two."

"Same."

"You watching Kuiksak?" Josh turned at the sound of Kevin's low voice. Josh hadn't heard or seen him come down the stairs.

"He's awesome," said Sam. "I think he's improved tons since summer camp."

Kevin sat down beside Sam. "Yeah, you know, I've been watching him too. He's a way better skater now. The guy is built like a rock. Did you just see that last hit? He nailed the guy."

Josh looked down the bench, surprised at Kevin's reaction. Was he for real? He'd never said anything nice about Peter before. Was this just for show? As hard as he looked, Josh could see nothing malicious in Kevin's face.

"Who do you guys play tonight?" Kevin was carrying on a decent conversation with Sam.

"Alaska," said Sam.

"They're so-so." Kevin leaned down and looked at Josh. "You guys play the winner of this game. That'll be Kuiksak's team, the way this game is going."

"Yeah, I know," replied Josh.

Suddenly, Kevin grinned. "You should see Alaska's pin. It's got this big dog on it."

"Are you talking about this pin?" Tony stood at the end of the row, his scarf draped over his arm. He proudly showed the pin to Sam and Kevin. "I think it's sweet."

"It's lame." Kevin laughed. "All the other cool ones have sticks or pucks that move. This one has a dog's tongue." He moved the tongue back and forth. "The LA Wave's pin has a gigantic wave that moves and it's awesome." Kevin kept moving the tongue back and forth, then he started barking.

Tony laughed. "Don't wreck the merchandise. I tell you, it's going to be the hottest pin by the end of the tournament."

"As if," said Josh.

Kevin glanced at Josh's empty scarf. "How come you're not trading?" Kevin pulled out his pins. "Here are the ones I got so far."

"I'm waiting." He stood tall, remembering Nick's speech about going to the gold medal game. There was no time like the present for Josh to practise being confident. "We're going all the way. Then our pin will be hot."

Sam playfully body-checked Josh. "The Kings are going to the finals."

"What about the Kelowna Stars, dudes?" Kevin flicked his hair. "We're going straight up the B side."

Suddenly, Kevin's name was called from up above. He turned and waved. "Gotta go." He flicked his hair one more time and took off.

"This game is almost over," Sam said to Josh and Tony. "Let's see if we can catch up with Peter."

Tony shook his head. "I'm going to stay here. I'll meet you in the lobby at one."

"Sure," said Josh.

The crowd broke into cheers. Josh glanced at the ice. "Hey, Peter has another breakaway."

"I bet he backhands it," said Sam.

"I think he'll take a wrist shot from the hash marks and shoot low."

Peter toed the puck and flipped it up, hitting the top shelf on a forehand.

"We were both wrong." Sam body-slammed Josh. "The guy got four goals."

Sam and Josh ran full speed down the stairs and headed out of the rink. While waiting for Peter in the lobby, Josh talked to Sam about school and hockey. Sam confided in Josh telling him that trying out for the Kanata team had been hard at first. Away from Becker, Sam seemed himself. Would being sort of famous make Peter a different person?

"I have a dog now," said Sam. "She's so cute."

"Really? I wish we could get a dog. Is she big or little?"

"Little."

"Hey, tell my dad you have a dog. Maybe he'll let me get one."

"Sure. Here comes Peter."

When Peter saw them, he headed straight over. His wet black hair stuck to his head like glue and his red face glistened in the harsh arena lights.

"Great game," said Josh.

"You crunched that guy." Sam's eyes widened and he grinned at Peter.

"Which guy?" Peter gave a quirky smile back, his dark eyes crinkling in the corners.

"Number 18, at the end in the third period. You ploughed him into the boards."

Peter let his equipment bag slide off his shoulder. "Oh, that guy. He was asking for it. He kept hooking me. Once he grabbed my jersey. The ref didn't call anything on him." Peter looked at Josh. "I hear the ref was slack in your game too."

"Yeah, I guess."

"I hear Bell should have been kicked out."

"I wouldn't go that far. He should have got a penalty, maybe. But kicked out? It wasn't that bad." Why was everyone talking about the hit? "We play you tonight." Josh shoved his hands in his pockets.

"Did you guys get pins?" Peter dropped his equipment and yanked a bag out of the pocket of his Edmonton Arrows jacket. "Ours are really big. I sent some to Tuktoyaktuk to my sister. I told her I'd send some of the ones I traded home too. She wants the one from the LA Wave team. To her it's like getting something from Hollywood."

Josh patted his pockets. There was no bulge from his bag of pins. And there had been nothing there when his hands were in his pockets. His pins were gone!

5 Dirty Hockey

"I lost my pins!" Josh turned his pockets inside out.

"I bet they fell out of your pockets when you were in the stands," said Sam. "Let's go check."

"I'll help too," said Peter. "Let me ditch my bag and stick first."

Josh watched Peter walk away. He was the most famous Bantam hockey player in Canada, but he still wanted to help find Josh's pins. He hadn't changed that much.

As soon as Peter returned, Josh started walking toward the doors leading to the rink. Within seconds he had broken into a run. He took the stairs two at a time to get back to the place where they had been sitting. *Yes, no one is in the seats,* thought Josh.

Josh got down on his hands and knees to search under the seats. No red bag. Then he searched the floor in the row in front. Next, he checked the row behind. Nothing. He stood up, pushed his hair off his face, and exhaled.

"I was sure they'd be here." He shook his head.

"Me too." Sam pointed down the stairs. "You could have dropped them between here and the lobby. Maybe they rolled somewhere."

"Let's check the stairs," said Peter.

"You guys looking for something?" Once again, Kevin had appeared out of nowhere. Josh noticed that Kevin hardly acknowledged Peter, giving him only a slight nod. But Peter nodded back anyway.

"Josh lost his pins," said Sam.

"Bummer." Kevin pulled out his scarf, which was heavy with pins.

Josh eyed Kevin. He didn't care about Kevin's stupid pins. How come he was always hanging around?

"I'm going to check down the stairs and in the lobby." Josh brushed by Kevin.

With Sam and Peter's help, Josh looked everywhere. But they had no luck. His pins seemed to have just disappeared.

"How could I lose them?" Josh shook his head angry with himself.

"I bet someone picked them up."

Josh squinted at Sam. "What did you just say?"

"Why are you looking at me like that?"

"Who has been hanging around us like crazy? Just showing up out of nowhere?"

"I don't know."

"Think about it." Josh's words came out in a rush.

"Kevin sat with us. Then he showed up again when we were looking for my pins. I bet he found them on the floor and kept them. He said he was going to get back at our team."

"That's dumb. If he wanted to get back at your team, he wouldn't take your pins. He'd smoke someone."

"But what if we don't play them again?"

"Do you really think he'd do that?" Peter hadn't said anything for the longest time. "Doesn't make much sense. He doesn't want to get a bad name at his own tourney."

"Yeah, but remember what he was like in the summer."

"How can I forget?" Peter rolled his eyes.

Josh's mind raced as he tried to think of how to handle the situation. What could he do to get his pins back from Kevin?

★ ★ ★

Mr. Watson talked hockey all the way back to the hotel. He'd watched some of the games and knew what teams were good, and what players to watch out for. Tony joined in the conversation, adding what he'd heard from some of the guys while he was trading. He even took a pen out of his pocket to write down some things that Mr. Watson said. Josh stared out the window, thinking of a plan to get his pins back from Kevin.

"Josh, you're not saying much," said Mr. Watson.

"Do I always have to say something? I'm listening." His dad couldn't find out that he had lost his pins. Josh would get the responsibility lecture, even though none of this was his fault.

Josh had his hand on the door before Mr. Watson had even parked the car in the hotel parking lot. "You boys are supposed to rest for an hour." Mr. Watson shut off the engine. "Then you have a team meal at four o'clock."

Josh hurried out of the car.

"Hey, wait up." Tony chased after Josh. "What's the rush?" he panted breathlessly.

"Promise not to tell anyone." Josh lengthened his stride.

"Tell anyone what?" Tony frowned at Josh.

"I lost my pins. And I think Kevin Jennings has them."

"What?" Tony pulled on Josh's jacket, forcing Josh to stop mid-stride.

"Are you sure it was Jennings?"

"Positive." Josh snapped his fingers. "I scratched my initials on the back of each pin. All I have to do is get his bag and I'll find my pins. I'll wait until after we play."

"But, what if it —"

"Shh." Josh didn't want to talk about it in public. They went through the hotel revolving doors and were greeted in the lobby by Nick.

"Team meeting in my room fifteen minutes before meal time. No swimming. Get rested and focused." Nick slapped Josh on the back. "Red, we need another great game from you."

★ ★ ★

The dressing room was quiet. Nick sat beside Josh. This gave Josh a boost. Nick could have sat beside his friends, some of the older guys, but he didn't. He made a point of sitting beside Josh and Tony.

"If we win again tonight, we don't play until two o'clock tomorrow. A lot of teams will be knocked out by then and just have exhibition games. That's not what I want for our team, that's for sure."

"Yeah." Josh could barely reply. His stomach churned with nervous butterflies. Winning wasn't going to be easy. He knew how good Peter was.

"What do you know about Kuiksak?" Nick asked, as if he'd read Josh's mind.

"He's tough. And fast. He gets tripped up easily."

"You mean knocked off his feet?"

"Not from a hit. He's sturdy that way. More from sticks and confusion. He's a rough skater and catches an edge every once in awhile."

"I think I get what you mean."

"If we play our game, we'll do okay," said Josh.

Nick smiled and looked Josh square in the eye. "We'll stop Kuiksak. With guys like you stepping up to the plate, we can win this entire tournament."

Josh sat tall. He was becoming part of this team in a big way.

The stands were fully packed. Josh stepped on the ice, nervous but pumped. He'd never played in front of a crowd this big. The tournament was a big event in Kelowna and it was as if the entire city had come to watch. Kelowna had just won a game and Kevin Jennings had scored two goals, so the hometown fans were in high spirits.

Josh skated at full speed in warm-up. Then he stretched out his back. He wanted to play exactly as he had in the morning game. Coach John put him on the second line but told him that, if he played well, he might get on the power play again.

First shift, Nick lined up at centre against Peter. The puck dropped. Peter managed to get control and send it back to his defence. Then he barrelled up the ice, looking for the pass. When the puck landed right on his tape, Josh sucked in a deep breath. It was dangerous to let Peter have the puck right away. Peter flew over the blue line, deked around the Rockies' defence, and wound up for a shot. The shot was like a bullet. Although the Rockies' goalie tried, he couldn't catch Peter's rocket shot.

First shift and Peter had scored. Josh stared up at the scoreboard. This was not good.

When Nick's line flew in for a line change, Josh stepped out. He saw the loose puck and raced toward it. He managed to get it on his stick, but one of the Edmonton Arrows was on him, lifting his stick, trying to throw him off the puck. Josh held firm. He gritted his teeth, grinding them against his mouth guard.

He pushed the puck forward and twisted his body to break free. Finally open, he accelerated to full speed with the puck on the end of his stick. When he saw his winger cross the blue line with him and rush to the net, Josh made a good hard pass.

His winger one-timed the puck. The Arrows' goalie whipped up his hand and snagged it.

Josh heard the guys from the bench cheering. "Great play!"

After one more whistle Josh banged on the boards to be taken off. His heart was beating rapidly in his chest. His legs burned. This was fast hockey.

"Good job!" Coach John gave him a pat on the shoulder. "Keep driving to the net."

Josh squirted some water into his mouth, then lined up on the bench to get ready to go back out.

The period ended with the Arrows leading the Rockies 1–0. Through sheer grittiness, the Rockies had managed to keep Peter Kuiksak to one goal.

In the team huddle at the beginning of the second period, Nick looked at everyone. "We only need one, guys, to be back at an even game. Let's keep stopping Kuiksak. And put one in the net."

Everyone put their hands in the middle. Josh could feel the energy radiating from everyone on his team for the cheer.

Every shift, Nick and Peter were on each other. Around the ten-minute mark in the second period, there was a big battle along the boards. Five guys were pushing and shoving, including Peter and Nick. Then Josh saw Nick shove his stick under Peter's skates. Josh looked to see if the refs caught what Nick was doing, but they were too busy yelling, "Play the puck!"

With a stick in his skates, Peter couldn't hold his balance. He fell to the ice, Nick managed to get the puck on his stick and took a stride forward. Peter quickly got up and moved to cut Nick off. He caught Nick along the boards and thrust his shoulder into him. Nick hit the boards with a thud, but somehow managed to push the puck forward.

Josh kept watching Nick and Peter along the boards instead of watching the path of the puck. Nick looked up, saw the refs were no longer watching him and stuck his stick in Peter's skates again. Peter stumbled, but quickly regained his balance. He whipped around and retaliated to the dirty stick work by cross-checking Nick back into the boards. Nick fell to the ice in a heap.

Peter wasn't as sneaky as Nick had been with Kevin. The whistle blew.

Peter got a penalty for cross-checking. At first Peter argued with the ref. Then he skated toward the box, shaking his head. Nick got up slowly and headed to the bench. Josh wondered if he was hurt. Usually Nick was the toughest guy out there.

Coach John yelled from his perch, "Power play, boys. Josh, I want you out. Nick take a seat."

Josh rushed onto the ice. Was Coach benching Nick? Or did he think he was hurt? Nick couldn't be hurt. The Rockies had to win.

Josh sucked in a deep breath as he lined up in the Arrows' end zone for the power play. This was his chance to do something big for his team. When his centre won the face-off and sent the puck back to the defence at the point, Josh moved toward the net. He kept his feet moving, trying to stay open. The Arrows' defence kept at him, but he just kept moving. The puck went over to the Rockies other defence, down the boards to Josh's opposite winger, then back to defence. When Josh saw his defence wind up for a slapshot, he got ready. The puck flew in the air and Josh stuck out his stick. The puck hit his stick, changed paths, and sailed into the net.

Josh jumped on his skates. He had deflected the slapshot for a goal!

His teammates crowded around him. Josh grinned

from ear to ear as they all patted his back. As Josh skated to the bench, Peter stepped out of the penalty box and skated slowly over to the Arrows' bench. His penalty had allowed the Rockies to score.

When Peter stepped on the ice for his next shift, he was on fire. He nailed Nick and sent him sprawling into the boards. *The guy can punish the body,* thought Josh, *and hard.* Nick got up and headed straight to Peter, who was ready for his defence to hit him with a pass. Nick tried to push Peter off his stick but Peter wouldn't relent. Nick kept jabbing and poking and pestering. Peter moved constantly. The puck skidded up the boards. Peter pushed Nick in an effort to get to the puck. Josh didn't think the shove was that hard, but Nick fell over Peter's stick and dove to the ice.

The whistle blew.

Peter had another penalty — tripping. He argued with the ref until one of his teammates pulled him toward the bench. His coach lost it, screaming, "Watch the dives Ref!"

By the way Peter slammed his stick when he got in the box Josh knew he was getting frustrated with Nick's cheap shots. Josh looked at his coach, hoping to be sent out again on the power play, but Coach waved to the line that was already on the ice and told them to stay out.

Nick won the draw and sent the puck to his winger. Then he crossed behind, headed to the outside lane, and tapped his stick on the ice for a pass. His winger hit his tape. Nick one-timed it. The puck hit the back of the net so hard the Arrows' goalie's water bottle fell to the ice.

The Rockies' bench went wild.

* * *

In the dressing room after the game, the guys on Josh's team screamed and yelled. Everyone talked about how the Rockies had a chance to win the entire tournament. As they talked, tingles surged through Josh's body. It would be amazing to go home with the trophy! Could the Rockies do it? Could they win?

Josh leaned back and closed his eyes. It was possible. They'd just beaten two of the best teams in the tournament.

Nick slapped his thighs and laughed, jolting Josh.

"I got Kuiksak so frustrated. Man, he was mad." Nick grinned. "First Jennings, now Kuiksak." He held up his hand to Josh. "Thanks for the tip, Red. Keep giving me the dirt, and I'll make sure we win this tournament."

Josh nodded, but half-heartedly. Nick was taking everything he said and playing dirty. Was that the only reason the Rockies were winning?

6 Tournament Talk

Josh and Tony left the dressing room and headed over to the other rink to watch the tail end of the Kings' game, even though they knew Sam was on the bench. The Kanata Kings were winning 6–2 and the game was halfway into the third period. Josh and Tony found an open spot by the glass to stand.

"I thought Coach John was going to bench Nick for the rest of the game," Tony said quietly as they watched Becker fly down the ice.

"Why would he have done that? He coached him last year and likes him." Becker rushed toward the net. For some reason, talking about Nick made Josh's stomach upset. He tried to change the subject. "Sam's friend Becker is good."

"Yeah, he's their best forward, for sure." Tony paused. "Nick is the Rockies best forward too, so he doesn't need cheap shots to be good. Do you think the coach might favour him a bit because he has a brother in the NHL?"

"No. He benched Nick for a shift."

"Nick's not playing the game like it should be played. He should just play like his brother does."

"He doesn't want to play like his brother. He wants to be different."

"He's being different, all right, but not in a good way."

"Let's not talk about Nick."

"The guy gives your team a bad name."

"It's your team now too," snapped Josh.

"Whatever." Tony shoved his hands in his pockets. "Have you thought any more about how you're going to get your pins back from Kevin?"

Relieved to be off the topic of Nick, Josh tapped his forehead. "I forgot about my pins. I was too busy thinking about hockey." He paused. "I think the only way to get them back is to somehow steal Kevin's pins and see if they're mine."

"But how?"

"I'll have to find out when he's playing and get in his dressing room." The crowd erupted as the Kings scored again. "Kanata is going to win." Josh looked up at the scoreboard. "We should go to the tournament table and check out the rest of the stats, see who we play tomorrow."

"If we win tomorrow, only five teams are left on the A side," said Tony.

Josh moved toward the door. "If we check the stats,

we can find out when Kelowna plays again so I can sneak into their dressing room and get my pins."

Tony groaned at Josh. "Let's forget the pin thing."

"No way," replied Josh.

The desk was crowded with guys reading the flow chart and the top-scoring chart. Josh and Tony pushed through until they were right in front.

"Can you imagine coming all this way and losing both your games on the first day?" Josh pointed to a number of teams on the list that were already out.

"They'll play games anyway," replied Tony. "My old team discussed trying to get in, knowing they'd be out right away. It's a great experience to just be here and play exhibition games against teams from all over North America."

Josh read the board. "Kelowna and Edmonton have to go to the B side because we beat them. We get a better schedule because we have won both our games."

"We're going all the way to the finals." Tony patted Josh on the back.

"You got that right." Josh kept scanning the chart. "Look," he whispered. "Kelowna plays at eleven o'clock tomorrow morning. Let's go find Sam. He'll help get my pins back."

Josh made his way through the crowd. A group of Arrows players stood by the concession.

"There's Peter," said Josh.

"He might not want to talk to us. We beat them."

But when Peter turned and saw Josh and Tony, he waved and walked toward them. "Hey," he said. "Good game."

"Thanks," replied Josh, a bit surprised. Some guys, like Kevin, would never say "good game" after a loss. They'd blame everything on refs or bad hits. "You played a really good game."

Peter shook his head. "I took too many penalties. I didn't handle that game the right way."

"You still have a chance to come up the B side." Josh certainly wasn't going to say anything about Peter's penalties, especially since he had been able to capitalize on the Rockies man-advantage and score.

Peter sipped his drink before he squinted at Josh. "And we will. We'll win that side and I hope we play you guys again. And when we do, I'm going to hammer your captain into the boards. He's a dirty dog. But I'll do it right, with a clean hit."

All the Nick stuff was getting to Josh. After every one of the Rockies' games, someone had something to say about Nick. Were they jealous? But Peter was leading the scoring race and had no reason to be jealous of Nick. Josh tried to convince himself that, with no penalties, Nick must be doing something right. All the convincing made him queasy.

"Your first goal was awesome," said Josh.

"Thanks. Too bad it was the only one I scored."

"You're still winning the scoring race by a mile," said Tony.

"Doesn't matter. I want my team to win."

Josh stared at Peter. The guy was sincere and definitely not out for just himself.

"Do you want to trade a pin?" Tony turned his pocket inside out to bring out a large pin. Fluff from his pocket was stuck to the pin. He blew it off and wiped the pin on his sleeve.

"Sure." Peter also pulled a pin from his pocket. He turned to Josh, "Did you find your pins?"

"No. I still think Kevin has them. I'm going to check tomorrow."

"How are you going to do that?" Peter asked.

"I thought I'd try to get into the dressing room."

"That's crazy."

"Not if someone stands out front." He playfully punched Peter.

Peter held up his hand. "Oh no, not me. I'm playing in the morning. Anyway, they lock the dressing rooms from the inside. It's too risky."

Peter was right. They did lock the dressing rooms. How hard could it be, though, to get a key from maintenance? Josh would say he'd left something in that dressing room.

"Hey, there's Sam." Tony whistled and waved.

Sam was lugging his massive goalie bag behind him. Becker was with him. Sam's hair wasn't wet, but

Becker's was soaked and his zits were bright red.

"You guys kicked butt," said Josh.

"Yeah." Sam nodded.

"You guys play Burnaby next," said Becker. "They have a little guy on their team who is fast and has great hands." He played with his stick to demonstrate.

Josh knew exactly who Becker was talking about. "Ricco," he said.

"He has a great skating stride," piped Peter. "I watched him yesterday, thinking we might play them today if we won. I'd do anything to skate like him."

Josh glanced at Peter. The guy was winning the scoring race by a ton of goals and he wanted to skate like someone else?

"One of the guys on our team," said Becker, "played against him in a spring tournament last year. He says the only way to stop him is to keep hammering him. And I mean pounding him. He hates cheap stuff and retaliates a lot. Then he takes bad penalties." Becker eyed Josh and Tony. "Talking about cheap shots, why is Bell playing so dirty? His brother doesn't."

"Cheap-shot isn't the right word to describe that guy," mumbled Peter. "He's the worst. I hate guys who play dirty. It'll catch up to him."

"I'm with you on that," Becker replied.

Josh didn't say anything to defend his team captain, although he knew he should. Nick had been great to him and helped him adjust to the AAA division.

"If we play you," Becker looked right at Josh, "I'm going to nail him good."

"I asked Coach if I could play that game." Sam looked serious. "I'll even sit two games in a row, but I have to play against you guys."

Josh jabbed at Sam, trying to lighten the conversation. "Yeah, well, I'll be ready. I know your weakness."

"Oh yeah, what weakness?" Sam's eyebrows pushed together. Could Sam be mad at Josh? They used to tease each other all the time.

Becker put his hand on Sam's shoulder. "The Kings' number-one goalie doesn't have a weakness."

Josh continued jabbing Sam. But Sam didn't play back. Josh dropped the playing around and shoved his hands in his pockets.

Peter pulled out a big Edmonton pin. "Anyone want to trade a pin?"

"I will," said Becker.

"My sister wants me to get as many as I can," said Peter.

Josh watched the guys trading. He had to get his pins back.

7 Even-Up Call

The next morning, Josh couldn't believe he'd slept so late. He had fifteen minutes before he had to head down for a team breakfast at ten. His dad had left a note that said he was in the restaurant with some of the other parents. Josh took a quick shower and towelled his hair dry. Tony showered and spiked his hair with gel. They left their towels in a crumpled heap in the tub, knowing someone would come in and clean up. When they left the room, Josh flipped the door sign to "Please, clean my room."

They entered the hotel restaurant and walked through to the smaller private dining room. Josh noted that there were just enough place settings for the team. A glass of orange juice sat in front of every setting. Josh sat down beside Nick and immediately drank the juice.

"I hope we get eggs this morning." Nick picked up a little butter tub from the bowl and started batting it around as if it was a hockey puck. "I love eating eggs before a game. They're high in protein."

"I'll eat anything, I'm so hungry," said Josh.

"With your diabetes, do you have to eat right away?"

Josh shrugged. "Yeah. But I just got up and I had a late snack before I went to bed, so I'll be okay. And I had juice."

Coach John stood up. "While we're waiting for our food, I've got a few things to say."

All the boys turned their attention to Coach John. "We don't play until two this afternoon, but I want everyone at the rink by noon. And I don't want anyone trading pins before we play, it's too distracting. I want you to sit together as a team and watch one of the other games. I don't care which game, I just want you to be together as a team. After we play, you're free to do what you want. We'll meet back at the hotel by six, and dinner will be in this room at six-thirty. If you want to swim you must do so in the afternoon and for no more than an hour. No evening swim, as we will have to play again tomorrow."

James put up his hand. "If we win today, do you think we'll have to play tomorrow? Maybe we'll get the bye and not have to play."

"We'll have to score a lot of goals to get the bye. There are five games on the A side today, and only one of the winners gets the bye. I think our focus should be on nothing but winning today's game." Coach John looked toward the door. A waitress walked in the room, carrying a big tray of meals, all the plates were covered with plastic lids. The smell of bacon wafted through the room.

Nick stood up. "Hey, team," he said. "We can win this tournament with or without a bye!"

All the guys cheered.

"That's the attitude to take." Coach John nodded in Nick's direction. "One game at a time. We win today, we move on. Now, enjoy your breakfast. You'll need the energy."

Josh ate his eggs, hash browns, bacon, and toast in about two seconds flat. He had checked his blood sugar when he got up and it had been a bit low, so he knew he needed to eat to get it back up to normal. When he had first found out he had diabetes, he had wondered if he'd be able to play hockey. It hadn't stopped him though. He found that if he ate properly and followed the rules the doctors had given him, he was okay. In fact he was playing the best hockey he'd ever played.

"Eat much?" said Nick. He still had toast left. He peeled back the foil on a packet of strawberry jam and scraped some onto his toast.

"It was good." said Josh. "I was hungry."

"We need to be hungry for another win today." Nick held up his hand. "And we're going to win!"

Josh smacked Nick's hand. Nick went back to his plate of food.

Josh pulled a loonie out of pocket and turned to Tony. "You want to play football?"

"You're on!" Tony piled his plate on top of Josh's and moved them to the side. Josh flipped the coin, but couldn't get it over the goal posts of Tony's hands. They played back and forth. Finally, Josh flipped the coin over Tony's hands to win the game. He threw his hands in the air. "I'm the champ."

"I'll play you," said James.

By the time Josh and James had finished playing, the rest of the team had surrounded them and everyone wanted to play. Nick checked his watch. "We have time for a short tourney. I'll make up the teams."

Writing on a napkin, he divided the team into pairs. The tournament was set up as single knock-out. Josh ended up winning his first game. Then he played Tony in his second match and lost. The waitress cleaned up the plates while they were playing. Tony and James ended up playing in the final game and everyone cheered them on. Tony won the game and was declared the champion.

"Okay, guys," said Nick, quieting the cheering guys, "time to get ready for our next big win! Let's meet in the lobby at eleven-forty-five."

"What time is it?" Josh asked Tony as they walked by the front desk.

"Eleven-fifteen."

"Drats,"

"What?"

"I forgot about getting my pins back from Kevin."

"I think you should just ask him to give them back." Tony frowned. "Your idea of going in his dressing room is really stupid. What if you get caught?"

Josh clenched his jaw as he tried to think. What would happen if a coach walked in and saw Josh rifling through Kevin's bag?

"Beat you to the elevator!" Tony sprinted away.

"No way!" Josh took off after Tony. Tony made it to the elevator first and pressed the button with the up arrow. During the ride up, Josh's thoughts veered to playing hockey and winning today's game.

The Rockies had a chance to make it to the final and win the entire tournament.

★ ★ ★

After watching Edmonton win 10–2, Josh and the rest of his team filed out of the rink to head to their dressing room. Rumour was that Kelowna had won their game too.

"I bet Peter wins the scoring race." Josh walked with Nick.

Nick stuck his hands in his pockets. "Yeah, a hat trick this game. I wish I was that good." He paused before he eyed Josh. "So … do you have any tips?"

"I don't really know anyone on the Burnaby team."

"I've heard that Ricco kid is good. I've also heard he's a hothead."

"Yeah, me too."

"I'm going to do to him what I did to your friend Kuiksak, make him mad so he plays like a dog."

Josh sucked in a deep breath. He wished that Nick would just play fair hockey, instead of always trying to bring down the best player. What if Nick got kicked out? The Rockies would have a hard time winning without him.

"Um." Josh wanted to tell Nick to play tough, not dirty, but he couldn't get up the nerve to say anything. After all, what if he jinxed their win by saying something that made Nick play poorly? Nick was their best player. And he knew exactly how to get the team pumped before a big game.

★ ★ ★

The puck dropped and, true to his word, Nick slashed Ricco. Ricco slashed him back before he chased after the puck. The pace of the game seemed faster than the last game. The stakes for the teams still remaining on the A side were getting higher. *If we can win,* thought Josh, *we're one step closer.*

He watched Ricco pick up the puck and smoothly stick-handle down the ice. The guy was good. Nick back-checked but couldn't catch him. Ricco crossed the blue line with the puck still on his stick. Was he going to try to shoot?

Ricco saw his winger on the far side and passed the puck. His winger one-timed it, but shot wide. The Rockies' defence managed to get the puck and fire it up the boards and out of the Rockies' end zone.

Josh got ready for the line change. He blasted on the ice and skated toward the puck. The Burnaby defence had the puck and Josh booked on it to get to him, trying to get him to make a bad pass. He swatted his stick in front of him. The defence glanced over, hesitated, and then made the pass. The Burnaby player flubbed the pass and Josh was able to tip it with his stick and send it sliding forward. He heard the bench yelling, "Go, Josh!"

Josh lengthened his stride. At full speed, he picked up the puck.

"Go!" He heard the roar of the crowd in the stands.

Josh cradled the puck on the end of his stick and skated toward the net. He was on a breakaway! He tried to think fast about what he should do. At around the hash marks, he wound up for a slapshot, letting the puck rip. He tried to aim low to the right side. The goalie slid over and stacked his pads. The puck hit the top corner of his pad and, instead of bouncing out, it bounced in.

Josh ran on his skates with his arms in the air.

His linemates rushed over and hugged him. All the guys on the Rockies' bench had their hands out, waiting for him to go down the line and slap their gloves. As he hit each hand, he could feel his blood rushing through his body. He'd hardly scored all year, and now he'd scored two in this tournament.

"Great goal," said Coach John.

"Thanks." Josh knew that under his helmet, his grin went from ear to ear. This was hockey!

The Rockies managed to hold on to their 1–0 lead until the end of the second period. In the dressing room, Coach John quieted everyone down by raising one hand.

"Keep it up, guys," he said. "You're playing good hard hockey." Then he looked directly at Josh. "Josh, if I had to give a number-one star for that period, I'd give it to you."

Josh's cheeks went hot as he nodded his thanks. His body quivered with adrenalin. He couldn't wait to get back on the ice.

"I want everyone playing tough hockey." Coach glanced around the room. He stopped when he got to Nick. "Tough hockey wins games. Let's keep it clean though. We won't win this game from the box."

Josh wondered if Coach John was on to Nick's strategy.

The third period started with as much fury as the

first. After Josh's first shift, he could hardly catch his breath. He came off and grabbed his power drink, taking a good swig before taking his position on the bench. He couldn't let his sugar get low or he'd be in real trouble.

As Josh watched, his elbows resting on the boards, he realized that Nick wasn't having his best game. He was out against Ricco every line, but Ricco and the Burnaby defence tied him up every time he got the puck. The Rockies' defence were playing awesome and stopping Ricco. But unlike Nick, who wasn't getting to the net, Ricco just seemed to be having a bit of a bad luck. Ricco hit the post four times, and Josh blew out a rush of air every time he heard the *ping*.

From the bench, Josh saw Ricco weaving his way down the ice. He bolted by one of the Rockies' defence. Josh sucked in a deep breath. If Ricco put it in, the score would be tied. The Rockies had to hold on to their lead to win this game. Ricco went wide and to the corner. Josh exhaled. Ricco was too far now to get a good shot away. Josh watched Nick skate toward him.

Ricco looked up, saw Nick approaching, and passed out front to his winger. Nick hit Ricco so hard the glass rattled. Ricco didn't fall. Then Nick chopped at his hands. Josh glanced at the ref, who had his eye on Nick. Why was Nick doing that? Ricco didn't have the puck anymore. Why was he taking such a chance?

If the Rockies got a penalty, Burnaby would capitalize on it for sure. Nick chopped again and hooked his stick around Ricco so he couldn't get to the net.

It was obvious, even from the sidelines, that Ricco was not happy. He shoved Nick's stick. Then the whistle blew! *Drats*, thought Josh. Nick was going to the box. The Rockies players moaned on the bench, knowing a penalty would hurt them big time.

Josh glanced at Coach John and noticed his teeth were clenched.

Josh looked back to the ice to see Nick chirping at Ricco. Josh could only imagine what he was saying to him. Suddenly, Ricco turned around and ploughed Nick in the face. The ref flew over and pulled him off Nick.

Then the ref sent both Ricco and Nick to the penalty box.

Beside Josh on the bench, James shook his head. "Nick's lucky that was an even-up call. That Ricco kid was stupid to retaliate on that one. Nick had the penalty."

"Nick's trying to make him mad," said Josh. "That's his plan."

"I know," replied James. "And it's a bad plan. I wish he'd just play hockey. Why is he doing this crap?"

"He wants us to win," said Josh.

"We can win without the garbage. He's giving our team a bad name."

Josh didn't want to believe what James was saying. Off the ice, Nick was a great guy. Nick just wanted to win his own way, to be different from his brother. Wasn't he?

Was he doing it the wrong way?

8 Bad Idea

"That's another one down!" Mr. Watson patted Josh on the back.

"Did you see my goal?" Josh asked.

Mr. Watson smiled. "Of course."

"It was such a good goal," said Tony. "You ripped it past the goalie!"

"I just checked on the Kanata game," said Mr. Watson. "They're up 4–2 and the game is almost over."

"They're still playing?" Josh immediately turned to Tony. "Let's go watch!"

"Before you take off, Josh." Mr. Watson held up his hand. "Did Coach John say what time you had to be back at the hotel?" Mr. Watson looked at his watch. "It's four now. If you want to swim, you have to do it before dinner."

"Dinner is at six-thirty." Josh glanced at Tony. "I don't really want to swim. Do you?"

"Nah. Forget Nick and those guys. I want to hang out at the arena."

Josh noticed his father had a funny look on his face.

"What's up, Dad?"

"I'm just wondering about Nick Bell. He's playing different these days."

"You mean, like a dirt bag," muttered Tony.

Mr. Watson tousled Tony's hair. "That's one way to put it. I'll meet you boys in the lobby at five-thirty."

As they walked away from Mr. Watson, Josh said, "It's not good to talk about your teammates that way. Coach always says to stay positive. That negative talk leads to negative play."

"Josh," said Tony. "You've got blinders on. Just because you hung out and met his NHL brother doesn't mean the guy can't and won't play cheap-shot hockey."

"He's a good guy."

"Off the ice, sure." Tony paused. "Someone should talk to him. Or at least talk to Coach and tell him to talk to him. I thought Coach John was going to say something to him after the game, but he didn't."

"Why don't you talk to the coach?"

Tony frowned at Josh. "I can't do it. I just got called up. It's not my place. Anyway," Tony paused for a second, "you've got a chance to be captain next year. This is your chance to prove yourself."

So Tony thought Josh had what it took to be team captain! Josh was pleased, but wondered if he could ever have Nick's confidence. "I'm not sure there's a problem," he said slowly.

"There's a big problem. The guy's going to get kicked out."

"You're overreacting. Come on, let's go watch Sam."

Josh and Tony ran into the other rink. The score was now 5–2. "They're up by three goals now. They'll for sure be the team to get the bye," Josh said.

"That means we'll probably play Prince George. They're giants. I saw in the stats book that they don't have anyone under 5' 10"? on their team."

"We have to be fast then." Josh knew he sounded more confident than he felt. He'd grown over the year, but he was still only 5' 3". The Prince George team was known to be as tough as they were huge.

"Hey," said Tony. "There's Kevin, on the other side." He pointed. "He's standing with that Ricco kid."

"They played together on a BC team last summer."

"They're pointing at us."

"It looks like they're coming this way."

"We should bolt," said Josh.

"No, let's stay. I've got an idea for you." Tony leaned in to Josh and spoke quietly so no one could hear. "I'm going to ask him if I can look at his pins. Then I'll somehow check the back of his Calgary pin to see if your initials are on it."

Josh held up his hand for a high-five. Now *that* was a plan!

Kevin approached them with, "Hey, looks like Kanata is getting the bye and you guys have to play Prince George, the tournament monsters."

"Yeah," said Josh. "Looks that way."

"I heard that Bell, Mr. Hotshot, was being a goon again." Kevin sneered. "His brother's probably disgusted with him."

"I wouldn't call him a goon," replied Josh.

"Oh no, he's not a goon," said Ricco. "Goons are a heck of a lot better to play with than cheap-shots. At least they just run you. I can duck away from those guys. Cheap-shots are like scum. You know, bottom fish who feed off anything. Why doesn't the guy just play hockey, like his brother?"

"He's a strategy player." Josh knew one of the roles of a captain was to keep the team together. He had to stick up for his teammate with these guys.

"Strategy player?" Kevin burst out laughing. "You're joking, right? Tell him we've got a strategy too. We've got the biggest guy from Prince George gunning for him tomorrow when you play them. The guy is 6' 3"? and can hit like Dionne Phaneuf from the Calgary Flames."

Josh broke out in a sweat. He really didn't want to hear about any of it. What was he supposed to do with threats like that? "I heard you guys won too," he said.

Kevin shoved his hands in his pockets. "Yup. We kicked butt. We're going all the way."

Ricco body-slammed Kevin. "We're on the B side now too. You ain't getting past us."

"And Kuiksak's team is still in," said Tony.

Kevin stopped horsing around with Ricco and frowned at Tony. "As if. They won't make it past either one of our teams."

Josh couldn't let that go by. "Peter Kuiksak is the best player at this tournament. He is way ahead of anyone in the scoring race."

Kevin scowled at Josh. *Good,* thought Josh. *That's the reaction I wanted.* Now if he could only get Kevin to admit he took Josh's pins.

Before he could say anything, Tony pulled out his scarf and looked at Ricco. "You want to trade?"

"Nah. I've already got one of your pins. I traded yesterday with your goalie."

The buzzer sounded to end the Kanata game.

"I'm out of here," said Ricco. "I've got to meet with my team to discuss *strategy.*" He gave Josh and Tony a smug smile.

After Ricco had left, Tony said to Kevin, "Got any new pins?"

"A few." He pulled his scarf out of his track-suit pocket. "Look at this one."

"Wow!" Tony glanced down at the scarf. "You do have way more than last time."

Was Tony pretending to be friendly because he was following through with their plan? He sounded so sincere. A wave of nerves washed over Josh as he wondered if Kevin could tell they were conniving.

"This one is radical." Kevin pointed to a pin that was shaped like a big rock. "It's from the Sudbury team. I like how the rock is rough."

"I don't have that one. Can I look closer?"

Josh held his breath when Kevin handed his scarf to Tony. Tony smiled when he looked at all the pins. "I want that Sudbury one," he said.

"They just played. I bet the guys are still in the lobby." Before Tony could look at the back of the Calgary pin, Kevin took his scarf back. "Come on," he said. "I'll find them for you."

On the way out, Tony glanced apologetically at Josh. Josh just waved his hand at him. Tony and Kevin bolted toward the crowd of guys in the middle of the lobby.

As Josh was waiting for Sam to come out, he saw Peter trading his pins. He walked over to the group and tapped Peter on the shoulder.

Peter swivelled around. "Look, I traded this one with Kevin." Peter showed Josh a Kelowna pin. "He's got a ton."

"The guy is such a jerk."

"Yeah, but he's an okay jerk." Peter shrugged his shoulders. "He's just one of those guys who acts super cool. I've got a few guys like that on my team."

Josh was surprised. Was Peter defending Kevin? Or was he just being a leader and refusing to bad-mouth other players?

"You guys won again," he said to Peter. He didn't want to hear how Peter liked Kevin.

Peter grimaced. "We started off slow."

"You're kicking butt in the scoring race."

"I guess. I'm on a good line. They pass the puck to me lots, so it's not hard to score."

Josh tilted his head and stared up at Peter. He was the opposite of Kevin who was all showing-off and bravado. Peter always deflected compliments he received to say something good about his team. Josh had read an interview with Sidney Crosby and noticed that he did the same thing. Maybe Peter really was headed to the NHL.

"You scored a nice one today," said Peter. "We watched part of your game."

"Yeah," said Josh. "But I had a good set-up too."

With a puzzled expression on his face, Peter said, "You're still not trading."

"Tony convinced me not to sneak into the dressing room to look in Kevin's bag."

"I think it was a dumb idea too. Are you *sure* he took them?"

"Oh, yeah. I'm sure."

Out of the corner of his eye, Josh saw Sam pulling his goalie bag into the lobby. "There's Sam," he said.

Peter smiled. "I'd love to put one past him. He's such a good goalie."

"His weakness is his five-hole."

"Really?" Peter frowned as if he was thinking. "I didn't notice that when I watched him."

When Sam approached, Josh held up his hand for a high-five. "Your team kicked."

Sam smacked Josh's hand. "I heard you guys won too. But a squeaker."

"It's still a win. We don't play again until tomorrow."

Josh hip-checked Sam. "Hey," he said. "Why don't you guys come to our hotel tonight? Do you think your coach would let you for an hour or so? I know my dad would pick you up and take you back to your hotel. We can play mini-sticks."

"I can ask." Sam grinned.

"I'll have to check with Mr. Patterson." Peter looked pleased to be asked, which made Josh feel good. Peter was the best player at the tournament and he still wanted to hang with them.

Josh went with his dad to pick up Sam at his hotel. Tony decided to stay back with some of the other guys from the Rockies. When Josh and his dad drove up to the hotel doors, Sam was ready and waiting. Becker was with him.

Josh slid open the side door of the van. Sam peeked in. "Is it okay if Steven comes?" Sam had a mini-stick and ball. So did Steven.

"Sure."

Sam and Steven piled into the Watson's van. It only took ten minutes to get to Peter's hotel. Josh was used to Calgary, a much bigger city than Kelowna, so the drive seemed short. Peter was also waiting out front, mini-stick in hand.

When they arrived back at Josh's hotel, he flung the van door open. All four boys raced into the hotel lobby and sprinted to the elevators. Josh won and pressed the up button first. They were going to press the button for every floor, but the elevator was full of people, so they couldn't. When the door opened at the third floor Josh flew out, running down the hall.

He swiped his key card and pushed open the door. Nick and Tony were sprawled out on the bed. Josh was surprised but happy that his two friends on the team were hanging together. "Hey, what are you guys doing?"

"Watching *Shrek*."

"That movie is hilarious." Steven bounced on the bed. "I love Eddie Murphy as Donkey."

"We're going to play mini-sticks in the hall." Josh also flopped down on the bed. Sam followed and started wrestling with Josh. They rolled over and knocked Tony off the bed. Nick hung on the sides of the bed, as if he was on a raft and didn't want to fall in the water. The bed cover slid halfway down the bed.

"Hey." Tony stood up and dove on the bed, creating a big dog-pile.

Josh started laughing. "Get off me."

At first Peter stood at the end of the bed, not sure what to do, but then he dove on top of the dog-pile. Suddenly, the door opened and Mr. Watson walked in the room. "Boys, you're making a mess."

Josh jumped off the bed. "Come on, guys. Let's play mini-sticks."

"We can play one goalie and two out per team," said Sam.

"I'll go with you guys." Josh gestured to Sam and Peter.

"Okay," said Tony. "Nick and Steven are on my team."

Peter's face suddenly clouded over. He glared at Nick. "Are you the captain of the Rockies?"

"Yeah." Nick stuck out his chest.

"Hey, guys," said Josh. "Let's play mini-sticks."

9 Hard Hits

The hotel hallway was too narrow for mini-sticks. Josh and Sam scouted for a good spot to set up the nets. They found an open space at the end of the hall where there weren't too many doors. Sam counted off twenty paces and set up the nets.

Josh went in net, as did Nick. Right off the top, Peter took possession of the blue ball, drilling it at Nick. Nick rolled to catch the ball, making a spectacular save.

"Pretty fancy," said Steven.

The ball was batted up and down the hall a few more times before Steven wound up and shot it at Josh. Josh tried to make a Hollywood save but the ball sailed into the little net.

"1–0 for the good guys," said Steven.

"I don't want to play net any more," said Nick.

"You calling it quits already?" Peter asked.

Nick ignored Peter and looked at Steven and Tony. "Who wants to play net?"

Tony shrugged. "I will."

As soon as the ball was in play again, Josh sensed the tension between Nick and Peter. They were fighting like crazy to get the ball, bashing each other in the shins and knees. One time they hit the wall so hard, Josh was sure someone would storm out of one of the rooms and make them stop playing. But no one did.

After an hour the score was tied 10–10. They'd had one break to raid the ice cube machine that was at the other end of the hall. The competition escalated, and Nick and Peter kept sliding on the burgundy carpet to get the ball. Nick had rug burns on his elbows. Peter's straight dark hair stuck to his forehead like wet paper. Sam kept wiping his face with ice cubes.

Josh was standing in net when he saw his father walking down the hall. *Yikes.*

"Boys," said Mr. Watson. "You're too loud. I think you should stop before someone reports you to the front desk."

"But it's a tie, Dad," said Josh. Sweat rolled down his chin.

"Okay. Next goal wins, but that's it." Mr. Watson put up his hand. "It's eight-thirty and I have to take you boys back to your hotels. I'm going to get my coat."

Josh and Tony agreed to go back in net. Steven had the ball and passed it to Nick.

Keeping low to the ground, Nick approached Josh. Josh got ready. Nick was winding up for a shot when suddenly Peter slid in for a tackle. Nick's stick flew out of his hands and his knuckles slid across the carpet. When he stood up he grabbed his hand. "That hurt!" He shook his fingers.

Totally ignoring Nick, Peter fired the ball in Tony's direction. Distracted by Nick, Tony wasn't concentrating on the game, so the ball went into the net.

Peter put his stick down. "Game over," he said. "We won."

With a scowl on his face, Nick shook his head at Peter. "That was a penalty. I think I should get a penalty shot."

"No way. You get away with shots like that in real games. Why shouldn't I get away with one here?"

"Shut up."

"Can't take what you give, eh?" Peter didn't raise his voice at all. "You should really learn something from your brother you know. He plays hockey like it should be played."

"I said, shut up." Nick moved toward Peter. Josh noticed that his fists were clenched. "Why do I have to be just like my brother?" Nick's face had broken out into red blotches.

"Because the guy is good," replied Peter. He still kept his cool. "Dirty hockey doesn't get you anywhere except in the box or suspended."

"I don't play dirty hockey, loser." Nick lifted his fist.

Peter held his ground. "What do you play then?"

Josh held his breath. Neither one was going to back down. *Peter has changed*, thought Josh. He might not be cocky about how good he was, but he certainly wasn't shy anymore. Were they going to fight?

Nick pushed Peter and he fell back against the wall. When Peter regained his footing, he glared at Nick. Should Josh stop them? His mouth was so dry, he didn't think he could get a word out even if he tried. He looked to Sam, who held his hands palms up and shrugged his shoulders. His eyes were the size of loonies. Then Josh glanced at Steven and Tony and they were standing like statues, just staring at the altercation. No one knew what to do.

Josh opened his mouth and was about to say something when he saw his dad approaching. Mr. Watson had his coat on. "Okay, guys, you ready to go?"

"We sure are, Mr. Watson." Sam spoke in an enthusiastic squeak.

"Yeah, I need to get back." Peter's low voice was the opposite of Sam's. "Um, I have a curfew."

Josh's shoulders sagged in relief.

★ ★ ★

Josh decided not to go along for the ride. After Mr. Watson, Peter, Sam, and Steven were out of sight, Nick kicked the mini-stick ball. "That guy is such a jerk."

"He's not a jerk." Tony picked up the mini-sticks.

"It was just a stupid game of mini–sticks."

Tony looked at Josh and mouthed, "Say something."

Josh folded up the nets and put them in their bag. As a younger year he felt funny saying something to Nick. Nick was a year older and the captain of the team.

"I'm going to my room," said Nick. "I want to watch my brother's game on TV. They're playing the Oilers."

"Yeah," said Josh. "I hope the Canucks win tonight."

In the hotel room, Josh flopped on the bed. "I thought they were going to have it out," he said to Tony.

"Yeah, me too," replied Tony. "Good thing your dad came out when he did." Tony picked up the remote and flicked on the television. Without taking his eyes off the screen he said, "You've got to talk to Nick. Remember what Kevin said — Prince George is going to goon him. He needs to hear that he has to play clean."

"Nick's not a bad guy." Josh kicked off the bed cover.

"I know that," said Tony. "He's fun. And I'd talk to him, but I can't. You know that." Tony finally looked at Josh. "You told me you want to be captain of this team next year. You should start right now, practising for next year." Then he gave a lopsided smile. "Maybe I can be your assistant."

Josh plumped up his pillow and leaned against the headboard to watch the game previews. Was Tony right about talking to Nick? Was this an opportunity for Josh to show he had what it takes to be captain?

"Do you think I should call his room?"

"I'd go see him."

"Okay." Josh sucked in a deep breath. "Here goes," he said, jumping off the bed.

"Good luck," said Tony.

As he walked down the hall, Josh's feet sank into the hotel carpet. He hadn't put on his shoes, and every step seemed to suck at his sock feet. His stomach felt like it was going to pop out of his skin. What if Tony was overreacting to all of this and was sending Josh on a pointless mission? The elevator door opened and Josh stepped out. No. He had to talk to Nick. Tony was right.

Josh looked at the arrows on the walls. He saw Nick's number, and turned right to head to his room. At the end of the hall, he saw Nick standing outside his room talking to Coach John. Josh turned and ran back to the elevator. He stood at the elevator door, thankful for a few moments to think about what he should say. He couldn't just tell the guy to play clean. He had to think of some other way to talk to him.

"Hi, Josh." Coach John walked around the corner.

"Coach." Josh turned and faked a smile.

Coach Josh patted Josh on the back, then pressed the down button on the elevator. "Tomorrow's a big game."

Josh nodded. The elevator door opened. "I'm going to Nick's room," he said.

Coach John stepped into the elevator and smiled. "You've been playing some good hockey, Josh." He winked. "We'll see you in the morning." The elevator door closed.

Josh sucked in a deep breath and made his way down the hall to the room Nick was sharing with Darren. He rapped on the door and tapped his foot while he waited for someone to answer. Nick opened the door in his sweats.

"What's up, Red?"

"Can I talk to you for a sec?"

Nick stepped outside, keeping one foot in the door so it wouldn't shut and lock him out. "What's up, man?"

"Um, I think we all need to play clean hockey tomorrow." Josh blurted out the words.

Nick leaned against the door, his messy hair falling over his eyes. His shoulders dropped and his face turned serious. "And what is that supposed to mean?"

"I don't think we need to take any cheap penalties."

"You're talking about me." Nick curled his lip.

Josh sucked in a deep breath. It was now or never. "Nick," he said, "you're the best player on our team. You're the fastest skater, you have the best shot, and you can score goals. You don't have to run guys or cheap-shot them after the play."

"I don't run guys. And I'm not a cheap shot."

"In this tournament you kind of have been."

"My brother never won this tournament."

"Who cares about your brother? You say you don't want to be like him, but all you do is spend time trying to be different or trying to win the wrong way to prove something to everyone who compares you to him. You don't have to do that." Josh stopped talking to catch his breath. Was he actually talking to Nick like this? Josh knew he'd opened a can of worms now so he had to continue. "I'd do anything to be as good as you, Nick. Not be as good as your brother — but as good as *you*. Except … I won't play cheap-shot hockey."

Nick shoved his hands in his pockets and didn't say a word. Josh wasn't sure if Nick was mad at him or not. Josh didn't like the silence at all, so he decided to change the topic. "What did coach want?" He asked.

"Not much."

"Oh." Josh didn't know what else to say.

"Um, actually, he told me I didn't need to gamble our game away."

"He's right." Josh paused, but just for a second. "I heard that there might be some big guys gunning for you. That's really what I came down here to tell you."

Nick frowned. "Who did you hear that from?"

"Jennings."

Nick pursed his lips as if he was thinking. He straightened his body to stand tall. Finally he said, "Red, thanks for worrying about me. I'll be all right." He patted Josh's shoulder. "You need to think about your game now, not mine."

Cheers erupted from inside the room. "Hey, Nick, your big bro just scored," a voice yelled from inside the hotel room.

"I have to go," said Nick. "Brent just scored."

★ ★ ★

"Hey." Tony glanced at Josh when he walked in the room. "What happened?"

"I talked to him."

"Did he listen?"

"I think so. Coach talked to him too. He was there before I was."

"That's good. You did the right thing for the team." Tony pointed to the television. "His brother just scored a great goal."

"Cool." Josh flopped down on the bed.

"Do you think Nick really will stop playing dirty?"

"I hope so."

"While you were gone," said Tony. "I was thinking about your pins. If you can talk to Nick, why don't you just ask Kevin for them and get it over with?

"I guess I could." Tony was right. If Josh could get the courage to talk to Nick, surely he could get the same courage to talk to Kevin. "I'll do it as soon as our game is over tomorrow."

10 Big Boys, Big Hits

The Prince George Rockets stepped on the ice for warm-up and Josh quivered. They were massive.

"They're huge." Tony got down on the ice to stretch beside Josh.

"We may be small, but we're fast." Josh said. He hoped he sounded more confident than he felt. He pushed one leg back to stretch his legs.

"You're not very convincing, Josh," said Tony.

A few seconds later, Nick skated by and patted both Josh and Tony on the pads with his stick. "Warm-up time, guys."

Josh glanced at Nick. He certainly didn't seem scared. And he was the one the gigantic Rockets were gunning for.

After warm-up, Josh helped pick up the pucks, then skated to the bench. Coach John leaned into the huddle. "Don't let their size scare you. We're fast. All you have to do is beat them to the puck and we'll win this game. Remember to break out of our end zone. That will be the key to this game, how fast you break out. If you're quick and don't slow down you'll beat them every time. I don't want to see anyone over-handling the puck. With a big team that could cause turnovers. They'll have long reaches. Don't play the middle, stick to the outside, and play give-and-go hockey. Make long passes." He stopped and eyed every boy on the team. "I want clean but tough hockey."

Josh glanced at Nick. He nodded his head at Coach John. Josh felt instant relief.

"We're ready," said Nick. He looked at everyone. "Hands in guys! Let's rock this place with our cheer!"

Josh had never been so pumped for a game before. If the Rockies won this game they would be in the semifinals!

Josh took his place on the bench as the first line skated to centre ice. Nick was paired with a guy who was at least a head taller. He bent over and placed his hand over his stick, ready for the puck to drop.

Nick won the face-off, sending the puck back to the Rockies' defence. The defence skated forward with the puck but, when he saw a Prince George guy coming after him, he threw a weak pass up the boards.

"You can't be scared," said Coach John on the bench. Josh kept whispering to himself not to be scared.

Nick hustled after the puck and a big Prince George player skated toward him. Nick picked up the puck and stick-handled, trying to beat him. Josh held his breath. Nick was going to get pounded. He should dump the puck or make a long pass. Josh snuck a glance at Coach John, who had a strained look on his face and was shaking his head. Then he looked down the bench and said, "I don't want anyone over-handling the puck."

Josh heard the crunch. The Prince George player had levelled Nick. He got up shaking his head and managed to give the guy a slash. Not a slash that would get a penalty, a slash to tell the guy to back off.

Every time Josh stepped on the ice, he wondered if he was going to get crunched. Prince George laid one hit after another. Every time Josh saw one of them coming after him, he took Coach John's advice and made a long pass or dumped it up the boards to chase. Twice he managed to pick it up and fire off a shot.

Late in the third period, the game was still scoreless. Josh came off after a shift, his chest pounding and his muscles screaming in pain. The extra hits were tough on the body and he was exhausted. He wondered how Nick was holding up. Every time he stepped on the ice, Prince George ran him and hammered him into the boards. He was definitely taking twice as many hits as any other player on the Rockies, but he was holding his own. He'd only had two penalties all game.

Josh moved down the line, knowing he was out again soon.

"We're scoring next shift," said Nick to his line-mates. They all smacked the boards with their hands.

Josh looked at the clock — two minutes left. If the game ended in a tie, they would have to play overtime, then there would be a shootout. Josh's line might get one more shift before the end of the period. If only he could score the only goal, the game-winner.

Josh watched Nick skate hard to the puck. By his stride, Josh knew he was determined. Nick's winger drove to the net. Nick managed to push the puck up the boards. Then he accelerated by a Prince George defenceman. The guy tried to hip-check Nick, but Nick was too fast. Nick had the puck on the end of his stick and was going to the net! Josh watched in antic-ipation. Nick skated two strides forward and took a look. A Rockies winger stood alone in front of the net.

"Pass out front," whispered Josh. The tension on the bench was high.

From across the ice, a Prince George player flew directly toward Nick. Was the guy going to board him? Josh cringed. Nick made a slick move and passed the puck right to the tape of the open man's stick. Then he did a sharp stop and turned toward the boards, head-ing around so he could catch a rebound.

The Rockies player in front of the net picked up Nick's pass and one-timed the puck. Josh heard the sound of the stick hitting the puck as it was shot low and to the far right corner. The goalie didn't have a hope of catching such a fast shot. Josh threw his hands in the air. The bench erupted in cheers!

Then Josh saw the Prince George player thrust out his arms and cross-check Nick from behind. Nick's head flopped and banged into the boards.

The bench hushed as Nick went down.

Josh stared at Nick, waiting, just waiting for him to get up and start chirping.

But he didn't get up.

He lay still on the ice.

11 Trusted Friendship

"Do you think Nick is going to be okay?" Tony's voice quivered.

"I don't know." Josh felt sick to his stomach and he couldn't stop shaking. The ambulance had arrived and the paramedics had taken Nick to the hospital on a stretcher. Josh and the rest of his teammates had stayed on the bench and watched until Nick was no longer in sight. Then Coach John had told them all to head to the dressing room. Josh was convinced that Nick was still unconscious because he hadn't moved at all.

The dressing room was quiet and still, as if the air had stopped moving and was hovering over everyone. Josh sat back and tried to stop his legs from shaking. What if Nick was hurt badly? The ref had kicked the Prince George player out of the tournament for cross-checking from behind.

When Josh heard the dressing-room door open, he sat up. Coach John entered, looking solemn.

"Listen up, guys." He spoke in a low voice. Everyone sat tall and stared at Coach John.

Josh held his breath. Was Nick okay? Was Nick not okay? What? He wanted Coach John to say Nick was going to play tomorrow.

"Nick's at the hospital and I've just heard that he has regained consciousness."

All the guys cheered. Coach John held up his hand to quiet everyone. Why did Coach John still look so serious?

"He will have to go through a battery of tests before they let him out of the hospital. He took a bad hit and the doctors want to make sure he's okay."

"Do you think he'll be able to play tomorrow?" The words just came out of Josh's mouth. He didn't know why or how he spoke out, but he did.

Coach John ran his hand through his hair and shook his head. "I don't think so." He made eye contact with every guy. "My feeling is that he'll be out for a few weeks."

Josh and Tony undressed slowly, then headed out to the lobby. The exhilaration behind their win had been lost with Nick going to the hospital.

"Do you think he has a concussion?" Tony asked.

"I don't know" said Josh. He paused. "He got smoked."

Josh saw Sam standing by the stats table with Steven.

Sam waved and headed over to him and Tony. Sam was watching the game today. He must have seen the hit.

"Is your captain okay?" Sam opened his eyes wide, as if he was shocked.

Josh shrugged. "He's at the hospital now."

"He got levelled," said Steven. "He probably has a concussion. He was out cold."

"Our coach told us he regained consciousness." Josh glanced at Tony. "But we don't know if he has a concussion yet."

"We'll find out later." Tony wiped some sweat off his forehead. "Probably when we get back to the hotel room."

"We just looked at the tourney chart. You guys play the LA Wave tomorrow," said Steven. He paused. "You can beat them." He smiled as if to cheer them up.

Josh nodded, but he wasn't sure why. Could they win without Nick? "Who do you guys play tomorrow?" Josh asked. He was trying not to think about Nick.

"We don't know yet," replied Sam. "There are a lot of games on tonight. My guess is we'll end up playing the winner of the game between Kelowna and Edmonton."

"What are you saying about Kelowna?" Somehow, Kevin had stepped into the mix of guys. "Man, Bell got smoked."

Josh glared at Kevin. Why did he always appear out of nowhere?

Kevin casually stuck his hands in his pockets. "Bummer for you guys. You will have a hard time winning without him. The guy might be cheap, but he can score."

Josh glared at Kevin. Nick had played tough, clean hockey against Prince George. "You'd like it if he couldn't play, wouldn't you?" Josh clenched his teeth.

Kevin furrowed his brows. "No."

"Give me a break," Josh replied.

"You guys are going down anyway. With or without him."

"You're the one who was all jacked that Prince George was going to go after him." Josh didn't know why he was talking to Kevin like that, but he couldn't stop the words from flowing from his mouth.

"He needed to be put in his place, not cracked into the boards with a dirty hit."

"You're such a liar." Josh glared at Kevin.

Kevin shook his head at Josh. "What's with you, man?"

"You told me you wanted him hurt. You were pumped that they were going to go after him."

"I didn't want the guy hurt, just hit hard. I wouldn't want anyone to get hurt. That's sick."

"Yeah, right." Josh balled his hands into fists.

"You're sick to even think I'd want that to happen."

"Shut up." Josh trembled. His insides were in knots. Nick had tried to clean up his act and look what had happened to him. Suddenly, Josh blurted out, "You took my pins didn't you?!"

Kevin's eyes bulged, his mouth opened, and his face scrunched up into a weird contortion. He looked totally shocked.

Josh was stunned by his own words. Why had he said that? He had planned to ask him, but not this way. Josh's body shook with fury and he wanted to say more to wipe the shocked look off Kevin's face. "I bet you've been trading them!"

Josh's face burned and his body broke out into a clammy sweat.

"What are you talking about?" Kevin frowned at Josh as if he was crazy. "Why would I want your pins?"

"When I dropped my pins in the stands a few days ago you picked them up and never gave them back." Josh stepped forward. Sam grabbed his sleeve to hold him back.

"Josh, relax," whispered Sam.

Josh's knees were shaking. His body trembled. Sweat ran down his back. He'd never really been in a fight before. He felt Sam's hand on his arm, holding him back. Sam knew Josh, knew he wasn't a fighter. He let Sam pull him back a bit.

"I never took your stupid pins!" Kevin yelled. "Why would I take them? I have my own"

"Josh," said Sam softly. "Let's go watch a game. The Arrows are playing."

"Yeah, why don't you go watch a game and cool down? I never took your pins!" Kevin stalked off.

"Josh, what the heck?" said Sam. "Why did you say those things to him?"

Josh felt as if he might throw up. "He shouldn't have talked about Nick like that." He paused to grit his teeth. "And I want my pins back."

Sam raised his eyebrows and shook his head. "I don't think he took your pins. And he definitely didn't want Nick hurt. He's not that bad a guy."

Josh looked at Sam. "Why would you take his side?"

"I'm not taking sides, Wattie."

Josh's shoulders sagged. Sam had made up the nickname Wattie for Josh years ago. He probably hadn't called him that since grade six. Sam was his friend, and nothing would change that. If it hadn't been for Sam, Josh might have got into a fight he probably wouldn't have won. He sighed. He had let his emotions get the better of him, and not in a good way.

"I'd forget about your pins," said Sam. "Especially when your team has a guy down."

"You're right," said Josh. He put his hand out, Sam grabbed it, and they did their old elementary school handshake.

For the rest of the afternoon, Josh hung out at

the hotel with his team. He played mini-sticks and Nintendo. None of the Rockies wanted to stay at the rink and watch games. They all wanted to be at the hotel to hear the news about Nick. They hoped there would be an update at the team dinner.

Josh had a strand of spaghetti hanging out of his mouth when Coach John walked into the back room of the restaurant. Josh slurped the spaghetti and gripped his fork. He tried to read the news about Nick from Coach John's face. And what he read wasn't good. The lines on Coach John's face were really pronounced and his skin looked white.

He stood at the front of the room. "Listen up, guys."

At first the forks dropping on plates created a clanging noise, then a horrible silence took over. It was as if someone had sucked the air out of the room. Josh couldn't hear anyone breathing.

Coach John ran his hand through his hair.

Finally, he looked at the guys and said, "Nick will not be playing for the rest of the tournament, or for another couple of months. He has a concussion and the doctors want to monitor it. And he broke some ribs."

Broke some ribs.

Everyone started mumbling to each other. Josh raised his hand.

"Yes, Josh," said Coach John over the talking. He sounded weary.

"Is he still in the hospital?" Josh remembered when

he had to go to the hospital for his diabetes. It had made him feel a lot better when people came to visit and brought him cards and presents. Hospitals were not fun.

The room silenced with Josh's question.

"No, he's out already," said Coach John.

"Maybe we should make him a card," said Josh. "We could all sign it."

"Good idea, Josh." Coach John paused and looked around the room. "Okay, some of you look defeated already. What happened is sad and not good, and I know how disappointed Nick is to not be able to play, but this doesn't mean the Rockies can give up. We're here to play hockey. We have a game tomorrow morning, and we're going to step on the ice ready and prepared to do what we can to take us one step closer to the gold medal."

Suddenly, the weird silence in the room was replaced with loud cheers. Josh stood up and pumped his fist the air. "Rockies, we can do this! Let's do it for Nick. Go Rockies! Let's win this tournament!"

12 Semifinal Game

Josh woke up at six the next morning, four hours before game time, unable to sleep another minute. His alarm was set for seven. He stared at the ceiling, thinking about being on the ice and skating, passing, shooting. If the Rockies won their semifinal game, they would go on to the gold-medal game.

News had trickled through the hotel about the other games. The Arrows and the Stars had both won, so they met this morning to see who would play Kanata in the other semifinal game. Prince George had lost again, so they were out of the tournament. Josh had joined in on the cheers when he heard that news.

The Rockies had to win today. They had to beat the LA Wave. The entire city of Kelowna supposedly came to the final game at the Prospera Arena. They'd put the score up on the jumbo screen and make announcements over the PA, just like they did for the Kelowna Rockets Major Junior team.

Josh's body vibrated. His stomach rumbled and he swore he could feel his nerves tingling. Could they win without Nick? Josh squeezed his eyes shut, trying to get any negative thoughts out of his head. They couldn't lose. They just couldn't. If they lost, they played for the bronze medal instead of the gold. Josh wanted to play for the gold!

On the ride to the rink, Josh stared out one van window and Tony the other. Josh didn't say a word. They didn't even talk to each other as they walked down the arena hallway. Josh's mouth felt as if chalk had dissolved in it, and he knew if he tried to speak his words would come out in mumbles. Entering the dressing room, he instantly noticed the weird hush. Who was going to replace Nick as captain?

When Coach John entered the dressing room, just before the start of the game, everyone was dressed. Coach took a moment to look around the room and make eye contact with every player. When it was his turn, Josh held his breath and looked into Coach's eyes with such intensity that sparks zapped his body. He shivered.

"I have confidence in every player in this room," said Coach John. "No team consists of one player and one player only. Collectively, we are a group. And yes, we're missing someone today, but each and every one of you has contributed to the Rockies' success so far in this tournament. If you play our game, we can beat this team." He paused to look around the room again. Then he raised his voice to yell, "Okay, get out there and play Rockies hockey!"

The room erupted in a frenzy of hoots and hollers. Josh was sure the entire arena could hear his team cheering.

Coach John held up his hand to try and quiet the team again. He obviously had one more thing to say. "For this game, I'm not going with a captain."

"I'm going with three assistant captains." He looked at Josh. "Josh you're the third assistant for today. We'll tape an A on your jersey. And I want you starting at centre."

Josh drew in a sharp breath. He could hardly believe his ears. He was being named Assistant Captain?! And centre on the first line?

With the black A taped on his jersey, Josh blasted onto the ice full of confidence. There was no way he'd let his team down. He fired off his shots in warm-up, sending them flying into the back of the net. When it was time to pick up the pucks, he was the first one to grab the puck bag. If he was going to be named a captain he'd better show proper leadership.

At the bench, Coach John stepped off the bench to be eye level with the team. "You can do this, boys! Remember, Rockies hockey wins the game. Okay, let's rumble this arena with our cheer."

Electricity surged through Josh as he lined up at

the red line. He had never been so nervous or so charged in his life. He stared at the puck in the ref's hand. He had to win this face-off. The LA Wave centre crouched low too. He stood at least ten centimeters taller than Josh. Josh didn't care, not today.

The puck dropped. Josh batted at it and managed to keep the Wave centre from passing it back. Josh's winger came in for support and got possession. Josh barrelled through the Wave players, trying to break lose, as his winger went wide. Josh crossed the blue line one step after his winger and headed directly to the net. But his winger got tripped up by the Wave defence. Josh screeched to a halt and swooped in for support. He battled along the boards, hoping to free the puck. Josh pushed and shoved, and kicked at the puck with his skate. The ref kept yelling, "Play the puck!"

When the puck finally was loose, Josh managed to pick it up. He lifted his head. Where were his teammates? He saw a Rockies jersey in front of the net! He fired off a pass — just in time, as he felt the body on top of him.

The puck landed on his teammate's stick. The Rockies' forward took a low hard shot that skidded along the ice, right under the goalie's pad.

It was in! Josh shoved the Wave player off him and rushed over to hug his teammate.

The Rockies had scored the first goal.

Back at the bench, Coach John patted Josh on the

helmet. "Great play. That's the way to hustle, Josh."

Josh grinned and took his place in line. The first period flew by and Josh was surprised to hear the buzzer sound to end it. It was still 1–0. Coach John gathered the team at the bench.

"Good period, boys. Defence, you've got a big job ahead of you. We want to maintain our lead. There can be no defensive breakdowns. No breakaways, no two-on-ones. If there are no breakdowns, they can't score. And we want to keep them off the scoreboard."

Coach John paused. "Forwards, you're on track. Keep it up. One moment of hesitation and there could be a turnover."

The ref blew his whistle.

Again, Josh got to take the face-off. This time the LA Wave player leaned into him, forcing him to lose balance. Josh lost sight of the puck in the scramble. The play headed toward the Rockies' goalie. Josh regained his footing, pivoted, and dug his edges in. He had to back-check, stop the guy. One stride, two strides, he was almost even with him.

As he bore down on him, he wondered what he should do. If he hooked, he took the chance of getting a penalty. Instead, he reached as far forward as he could and stuck his stick under his opponent's stick. The lift was enough to make the player hesitate and lose his stick-handling rhythm. Josh didn't have a long enough reach, however, to grab the puck.

The play continued in the Rockies' end for another twenty seconds. Josh's legs were dying. He had to get off. But he couldn't until the Rockies were out of their own end. He heard Coach John yelling from the bench. "Clear the puck! We need a line change."

Finally, the Rockies' defence got the puck up the boards and over the blue line. Josh skated over to the bench.

As soon as Josh hit the bench, a Rockies player flew out. Josh sat down and put his head between his legs. His heart thumped. His breathing was rapid. Once he had caught his breath, he sat up and swigged some water.

"Go!" His teammates yelled from the bench.

Josh quickly stood. Tony was on a breakaway! "Come on, Tony," said Josh to himself. "You can do it."

Tony skated toward the net. Was he going to shoot or deke? "Go low," whispered Josh.

Tony must have heard Josh because he deked, then fired off a hard low snap shot. The puck zinged by the goalie and bounced off the net to land behind the line. Josh cheered from the bench. Tony fell to one knee and pumped his arm. Then he flew over to the bench to slap hands with every player.

The Rockies were now up 2–0.

The Wave managed to squeak in one goal late in the third period, but it wasn't enough to take the win. When the buzzer went to end the game, the score was

2–1 for the Rockies. Josh hopped over the boards and raced to his goalie and joined his teammates as they circled him. They had decided in the dressing room to save the dog-pile until the last game — when they won the championship.

In the dressing room, Josh unsnapped his helmet and took it off. There was not one hair on his head that wasn't dripping in sweat.

He turned to Tony and grinned. "We won! You scored the winner!"

"I can't believe I scored." Tony's eyes shone.

"It was such an awesome goal." Josh leaned back. "We're going to the finals." All the nervous energy he'd had before the game had turned to elation.

"I wonder who we'll play." Tony tossed his shoulder pads into his bag.

"Arrows beat Kelowna this morning, so either Peter's team or Sam's team. They play off this afternoon." Josh untied his skate, wiped the blade with a rag, and slipped the cloth cover on for protection. When he looked at Tony, he couldn't help but smile. "I'm so glad Edmonton kicked the crap out of Kelowna."

"They didn't really kick the crap out of them. The score was 2–2. It went into overtime then a shoot-out."

"Yeah, and Kuiksak scored and Jennings missed." Josh slapped his thighs.

Tony chuckled. "Jennings probably went ballistic afterwards."

"Probably." Josh was finally undressed. "Kuiksak is going to win the scoring race, hands down. I wonder if he'll win tournament MVP too."

Tony didn't answer Josh because he was searching for something in his hockey bag. "Have you seen my jacket?" he said quietly.

Josh shook his head. "Didn't you wear it this morning?" Josh couldn't remember what Tony had on before the game. He had been too focused and nervous.

"I couldn't find it. I looked everywhere in the hotel room when you were in the shower. And I looked in the back seat of the van, but it wasn't there either. I hoped it was in my bag but it's not." Tony had a look of panic in his eyes. "I have to find it. We're watching the Kings/Arrows game as a team tonight and we all have to wear our track suits. And I need it for tomorrow. It's our team uniform. I can't be without my jacket for the gold-medal game."

James, who was sitting beside Tony, stood up and put on his jacket. Then he put on his hat. "I lost my team hat the other day and found it in a lost-and-found box they have by the stats table."

Tony crossed his fingers. "Let's hope it's there. Come on Josh, let's go."

The woman running the stats desk showed Josh and Tony the big box. It was heaped with T-shirts, sweat pants, jackets, hats, gloves. Tony started rifling through it.

"Here, take some of the stuff out," said Josh. "We can always put it back in."

One by one, they removed articles of clothing from the box. They were almost at the bottom and still there was no jacket.

"It's got to be here." Tony pulled out yet another smelly T-shirt.

"What are you boys looking for?" Mr. Watson's voice sounded from the distance.

Josh stood up right away. "Tony lost his —" Josh stopped and grinned. Mr. Watson held Tony's jacket in his hands.

"I found it under the front seat of the van," he said.

"Awesome! Thanks, Mr. Watson." Tony took his jacket and put in on.

"Make sure you put everything back in that box." Mr. Watson pointed to the mess on the floor. Then he turned and walked away.

"Come on, Tony," said Josh. "Help me."

Josh grabbed a heap of clothing and, just as he was tossing it into the box, he saw something familiar. He threw the clothes on the floor and reached into the box, pulling out a red bag full of pins.

13 Check and Cross-Check

"Are you going to tell Kevin you found your pins?" Tony asked.

Josh had checked the back of one of the pins to verify that it was indeed his bag. "I don't know. Should I?"

Tony shrugged. "You could just let it go." He paused. "But you did accuse him of stealing them."

"I know."

"We should have checked the lost-and-found."

"I was convinced Kevin took them." Josh ran his finger along the soft felt. "I feel like a big idiot now. Why didn't I check the box? When I lose something at home, my mom always goes through every step. She says you have to check and cross-check if you want to find things."

"Uh-oh. There's Kevin now." Tony pointed across the room. "Hide your pins."

Josh moaned. "I can't." He waved when Kevin looked in his direction.

Kevin had definitely noticed the bag. He strutted over to Josh. "Where did you find your pins?"

"In the lost-and-found," said Josh sheepishly.

"I told you I didn't take them."

"Sor-ry." Josh grimaced. How mad was Kevin? He was a funny guy to read. Josh thought he'd be cranked.

Kevin's scowl suddenly changed to a big grin. "Hey, Dude, I think you owe me a couple of free pins for that."

So that's why he isn't too mad; he has another agenda, thought Josh. Josh knew he had to comply. He opened his bag and handed Kevin two of his big pins. When Kevin snapped his fingers, wanting more, Josh reached in his bag and pulled out two small ones. He shook his head at Kevin.

Kevin just smirked back. "You know you owe me."

Josh rolled his eyes, then cracked a smile. He did owe Kevin.

Kevin playfully punched Josh on the shoulder. "Good luck tomorrow!" He held up the big Rockies pin. "You win tomorrow and I'll have the best pin collection of anyone in this tourney. Somehow, someway, I'm going home a winner."

Josh's smile dissolved in his laughter.

★ ★ ★

Josh sat in the stands in between Nick and Tony, watching Kanata and Edmonton battle it out. Nick had refused to go home even though his ribs were bandaged and it hurt him to laugh.

The game was fast-paced and the play seemed to be going up and down the ice like a tennis ball bouncing back and forth over a net. Both teams knew what was riding on the outcome. A win was berth in the gold-medal game.

"Here comes Kuiksak on a breakaway!" Josh pointed.

"The guy's like an army tank," said Tony. Since Tony had scored his goal in the last game, he seemed so much more relaxed and part of the team. The guys were really accepting him. Josh was happy for him.

"I bet he wins MVP," said Nick.

Josh snuck a glance at Nick. Poor guy. It would be so hard to have to sit and not play when your team was in the gold-medal game.

Peter blasted a shot at Sam. Sam threw his hand in the air and grabbed the flying puck. He snapped his glove shut. The whistle blew. Sam shook his hand.

"I bet that stung," said Nick.

"He should have gone to his five-hole," said Josh. "That's Sam's weakness."

"His butterfly looks good to me."

"Believe me," said Josh. "I've played with Sam for years. He's got a weak five-hole."

The teams lined up for a face-off. Peter won the draw, looked up, and passed to his winger, who fired on Sam. Sam made an unbelievable save by stacking his pads.

"Kuiksak plays such solid hockey," said Tony. "He's not a dirty player at all. He just does everything right."

"I'm playing that way when I come back."

Josh looked at Nick. "As soon as you get back, the Rockies are going to be unstoppable. I bet we win the cities," said Josh.

"Let's win tomorrow first." Nick gave Josh the thumbs-up.

Josh held up his hand for a high-five but Nick shook his head.

"It hurts to lift my arm."

Josh turned and hi-fived Tony once then twice. "Second one was for you Nick," he said.

The Kings beat the Arrows 6–5. Peter had scored another hat-trick but it wasn't enough. Out in the lobby, Josh and Tony waited for Sam. They weren't sure if Peter would want to talk after losing such a big game.

When Sam came out, he was all smiles. He immediately headed for Josh and Tony.

"I guess we play you tomorrow," said Josh.

Sam bobbed his head. "I guess so." His eyes lit up with excitement. "Coach just told me I'm playing too."

"It will be a heck of a game."

"We're going to kick your butt," Steven piped up.

"No, we're going to kick yours." Josh laughed.

They horsed around for a few more minutes, bantering back and forth about who was going to win the game. Sam grinned. "I heard you found your pins, Loser." He shook his head at Josh. "Why didn't you check the lost-and-found right away?"

"You could have suggested it too you know."

"They weren't my pins."

Josh pulled out his bag. "You want to trade?"

"Nope, I'm waiting until tomorrow."

"But yours won't be worth anything tomorrow."

"We'll see about that."

Josh grinned. "Yeah, we'll see about that." Out of the corner of his eye, he saw Peter walking through the arena lobby. "I bet Kuiksak wins tourney MVP and high scorer."

"Oh, yeah," said Sam. "He blasted three by me today. Two of them I didn't even see."

Josh saw Peter look in his direction so he lifted his hand and gave a little wave, wondering what his reaction would be. Would he want to talk? Or just go home?

As soon as he saw Josh and the gang, Peter walked over.

"Hey," said Josh. "Great hat trick."

"Thanks." Peter dropped his bag off his shoulder and it landed with a thud. Then he rested his chin on his stick. He turned to Sam and Steven. "Good game."

"Thanks," said Sam. "You guys will win the bronze medal for sure."

"Yeah." Peter tried to smile but only one corner of his mouth lifted. "Burnaby is good though. We can't take the game too lightly. That Ricco is fast." He looked at the red bag in Josh's hands. "Did you find your pins?"

"In the lost-and-found."

The corners of Peter's mouth lifted. "Are you kidding? Does Kevin know?"

"Yeah. I had to give him two big ones and two little ones."

Peter laughed. "That'll teach you."

Yeah, that will teach me, thought Josh.

14 Gold-Medal Game

The arena was jammed to capacity. Josh tried not to stare at the crowd. The noise seemed to reverberate off the concrete walls. He skated around the net and up to the blue line, then he dropped down to stretch. His stomach churned. When he glanced over at the Kanata end, he saw Sam warming up. He had to look away. It felt so weird playing against Sam, especially in such a big game.

After the warm-up, the Rockies huddled at the bench. Coach John leaned into the group. "Remember, play our game. I want an aggressive offence with two men high."

Josh sucked in a deep breath, trying to stop the butterflies swarming through his stomach.

The Rockies cheer was the loudest it had ever been. With his ears still ringing, Josh skated to centre ice. He leaned over and stared at the puck. As soon as it left the ref's hand, he moved. When he saw it on the end of his stick he batted it back. He had won the first face-off. His defence picked it up and passed it up the boards. His right winger picked it up and hustled forward. Josh drove to the net.

But the winger was picked off at the blue line. The turnover made Josh slam to a halt and change directions. Now the Kings were in control and heading toward the Rockies' net. Josh back-checked, hoping to stop the Kings from penetrating the Rockies' end. But the Kings kept possession of the puck, passing it around in the Rockies end. Josh kept looking for a chance to steal the puck, to get it out of the Rockies' end zone. He batted and poked and fought hard along the boards. Finally, the Kings took a shot on net. It was a weak shot, easily saved by the goalie.

Josh saw his gate open — time for a line change. He skated to the bench. One shift and he was totally out of breath. Coach had told them to make every shift count and keep them short.

Shift after shift, Josh skated up and down the ice.

With less than two minutes left in the second period the game was still scoreless. Josh stepped on the ice and glanced at the clock. This could be his last shift before the end of the period. He'd had a few chances to score, but he certainly wasn't creating opportunities like he should. In fact, every shot he'd made had been to Sam's glove hand. No one could get one in on Sam's glove hand, Josh knew that. Sam was playing unbelievably well. Josh had to get the puck low on Sam. Determined to make his last shift in the period count, Josh lined up just outside the blue line for the face-off.

Josh controlled the puck and sent it flying over the blue line. He'd been winning his face-offs all game. Sometimes he sent the puck back, but he knew it was important to get the puck in the Kings' end zone. His wingers were supposed to be prepared to rush to the puck. But this time a quick Kings defence got to the puck first.

Josh sprayed snow with his stop and skated back. The Kings headed in, but the Rockies' defence stopped the play, creating a turnover. Again Josh stopped, spraying snow and shifting his weight to go the other way. He raced forward, looking for the pass. His legs screamed, but still he skated harder. When the puck landed on his tape, he lengthened his stride. He glanced around, saw his winger, and fired the puck forward. Then he drove to the net. His winger cycled the puck back to the defence and the defence sent it back to the winger. Josh moved around, trying to remain open. His winger passed it to him, and Josh one-timed it. Again, his shot went too high. Sam stuck out his glove and snatched it from the air. This was crazy. Josh had to shoot low, to Sam's five-hole, to his weakness.

Both teams filed to the dressing room between the second and third period.

"I keep shooting too high," he said to Tony.

"Yeah, me too. Sam stones me every time."

"Next period," said Josh. "I'm going low. We can win this game."

The third period started and the pace was faster and more furious. After thirty seconds on the ice, Josh was done. He would have to change on the fly. Coach John had told them in his pep talk to keep the shifts short so they had legs to drive to the net.

Josh was puffing when he took his place on the bench. Breathing deeply, he watched the action on the ice. James almost created a breakaway, only to get the puck tangled in his feet. Next shift Josh would create a scoring opportunity. He had to.

But on his next shift it didn't happen. The puck bounced and neither team did anything with it. When it was his turn to come off, he felt his line had had a bad shift.

"We've got to shoot!" Coach John yelled from his perch. "Drive to the net. Play offensively."

Josh nodded.

A couple of times Josh's line was close to scoring, but they couldn't quite get the puck in the goal. And a couple of times the Kings were close to scoring, but they couldn't either.

With two minutes left to play, the score was still 0–0. Josh knew the first goal would win the game.

He flew out of the gate and headed to the puck.

This was *his* shift. He was going to create an opportunity to score. The Kings were heading down the ice with the puck. Josh managed to get in line with the Kings' winger and centre. If the winger passed to the centre, Josh might be able to pick off the pass. In his head, Josh tried to figure out where the puck would end up if passed over. He had to anticipate, be ready.

Sure enough, the Kings player passed over. Josh stuck his stick out, hoping to touch it, make it change directions. The puck deflected off his stick! He reached and managed to get it on his stick. He pushed it forward.

Could he hold on to the puck?

Somehow, luck was with him. The puck didn't get tangled in his skates. It stayed on his stick. If he could just get ahead by a few strides, he'd open up. He heard the crowd screaming for him to skate. He dug in hard and pushed with his legs. *Accelerate, Josh, accelerate.* He heard the Coach's voice in his head. He pushed the puck ahead and skated as hard as he could.

He skated like he'd never skated before.

He took a split second to look around. No one was with him. He was on a breakaway! Now the only person between him and the net was Sam.

Josh barrelled toward Sam. He didn't have to do anything fancy to put one by Sam. Josh knew his weakness. All he needed to do was fire a low hard shot to the five-hole. Josh saw Sam's five-hole and blasted the puck at him.

He knew it was a zinger. He knew it was accurate too.

Sam sank into a butterfly. The puck bounced off his pads, landing out front. Josh raced in for the rebound but Sam dove forward, slapping his glove on the ice. He ducked his head and held on to the puck. Josh was going so fast, he flew over Sam and crashed into the back of the net.

The whistle blew. Josh detangled himself and got up. Then he smacked his stick on the ice. How could he have missed? He had a chance to put his team ahead and had blown it. He quickly looked up at the scoreboard. The 0–0 score and the 1:20 remaining on the clock made him feel sick to his stomach. Shoulders slumped, he skated to the bench.

Coach John patted him on the back. "Good try Josh. Sam's got a good butterfly. The best way to beat him is in a deke."

Josh sucked in a deep breath, willing himself to get over his mistake. Sam might not have changed off the ice, but he had changed on the ice. Why hadn't Josh noticed? He shook his head. He had to focus. There were precious few seconds left in the game.

As Josh watched both teams battle it out, he also watched the clock. It ticked down. One minute left. Then fifty-nine seconds. The Rockies had control. They'd have to go to overtime.

Suddenly, the puck overturned. Steven broke

though the Rockies' defence. He headed down the ice. Josh held his breath. Steven wound up for a shot, then faked the shot and deked. The Rockies' goalie slid across the net and sunk into his splits. The puck clipped the top of his pad and took a bad bounce. It landed just behind the line.

The Kings went crazy.

The Rockies fell silent.

At the end of the game, the score was 1–0 Kings. Although Josh tried to be brave, a tear escaped from the corner of his eye. He quickly wiped it away. He noticed James doing the same thing.

Both teams lined up at the blue line for the medal presentation. When they put the silver medal around Josh's neck he didn't even look at it. Silver was no consolation.

The announcer voice boomed through the PA system. "Now it's time for our awards." He paused to pick up a trophy.

"The tournament rookie award sponsored by the Kelowna Rockets is awarded to... Josh Watson from the Calgary Rockies!"

Josh couldn't believe his ears. He never won awards. Ever.

"Go, Josh," said Tony.

Josh skated to the trophy table and shook hands with the Mayor of Kelowna. Then he posed for a picture.

With his trophy in hand, Josh skated back to his spot in line.

"Way to go," said Tony.

Josh smiled from ear to ear.

Tony pointed to the bench. "Kuiksak's on the bench dressed in street clothes. The Arrows won the bronze medal. I bet he's on the bench because he gets the MVP award."

"He's top scorer too. No one came close to him."

The announcer picked up another trophy. "And the tournament goalie award goes to ... Sam Douglas from the Kanata Kings!"

Josh smacked the ice with his stick when Sam skated forward to accept his award. He had his mask up and Josh could see the grin on his face. Sam deserved his award.

"Sam made a great save on you," said Tony to Josh.

"I blew it."

"His butterfly has improved *so* much."

"I thought I knew his weakness." Josh watched Sam pose for his picture. His face was beet red and his smile as wide as the Bow River in Calgary.

Tony shook his head. "It's not his weakness any more. We should have checked him out more closely during the previous games."

Josh nodded. "You got that right. You may not be allowed to cross-check on the ice, but you sure have to cross-check off the ice to get things right. I got stung twice this tourney."

"Just don't go for the hat trick." Tony laughed.

"Don't worry. I'll save my hat trick for our next game," replied Josh.

Other books you'll enjoy in the Sports Stories series

❏ *Power Play* by Michele Martin Bossley
An early-season injury causes Zach Thomas to play timidly, and a school bully just makes matters worse. Will a famous hockey player be able to help Zach sort things out?

❏ *Danger Zone* by Michele Martin Bossley
When Jason accidentally checks a player from behind, the boy is seriously hurt. Jason is devastated when the boy's parents want him suspended from the league.

❏ *A Goal in Sight* by Jacqueline Guest
When Aiden has to perform one hundred hours of community service, he is assigned to help a blind hockey player whose team is Calgary's Seeing Ice Dogs.

❏ *Ice Attack* by Beatrice Vandervelde
Alex and Bill used to be an unbeatable combination on the Lakers hockey team. Now that they are enemies, Alex is thinking about quitting.

❏ *Red-Line Blues* by Camilla Reghelini Rivers
Lee's hockey coach is only interested in the hotshots on his team. Ordinary players like him spend their time warming the bench.

❏ *Goon Squad* by Michele Martin Bossley
Jason knows he shouldn't play dirty, but the coach of his hockey team is telling him otherwise. This book is the exciting follow-up to *Power Play* and *Danger Zone*.

❏ *Interference* by Lorna Schultz Nicholson
Josh has finally made it to an elite hockey team, but his undiagnosed type one diabetes is working against him — and getting more serious by the day.

❏ *Deflection! by Bill Swan*
Jake and his two best friends play road hockey together and are

members of the same league team. But some personal rivalries and interference from Jake's three all-too-supportive grandfathers start to create tension among the players.

❏ *Misconduct* by Beverly Scudamore
Matthew has always been a popular student and hockey player. But after an altercation with a tough kid named Dillon at hockey camp, Matt finds himself number one on the bully's hit list.

❏ *Roughing by Lorna Schultz Nicholson*
Josh is off to an elite hockey camp for the summer, where his roommate, Peter, is skilled enough to give Kevin, the star junior player, some serious competition, creating trouble on and off the ice.

❏ *Home Ice* by Beatrice Vandervelde
Leigh Aberdeen is determined to win the hockey championship with a new, all girls team, the Chinooks.

❏ *Against the Boards* by Lorna Schultz Nicholson
Peter has made it onto an AAA Bantam team and is now playing hockey in Edmonton. But this shy boy from the Northwest Territories is having a hard time adjusting to his new life.

❏ *Delaying the Game* by Lorna Schultz Nicholson
When Shane comes along, Kaleigh finds herself unsure whether she can balance hockey, her friendships, and this new dating-life.

❏ *Two on One* by C.A. Forsyth
When Jeff's hockey team gets a new coach, his sister Melody starts to get more attention as the team's shining talent.

❏ *Icebreaker* by Steven Barwin
Gregg Stokes can tell you exactly when his life took a turn for the worse. It was the day his new stepsister, Amy, joined the starting line-up of his hockey team.

❏ *Too Many Men* by Lorna Schultz Nicholson
Sam has just moved with his family to Ottawa. He's quickly made first goalie on the Kanata Kings, but he feels insecure about his place on the team and at school.